DREAMS OF DUST

JAMES AGEE JR.   CHRIS MANNING   ADAM ROSE

KATIE JOHNS   DAMIAN STEVENSON

LORRAINE BRADNER

Treasure Ink Press

Cover Design: James Agee Jr.

Editor: Katie Johns

ISBN: 9798839299542

CONTENTS

The Pond by James Agee Jr.

The Pond is an exclusive body of water that offers magnificent healing powers for those who can afford to visit. One struggling family has faced hardship and saved to be able to visit The Pond, but is it truly everything that they thought it would be?

Meet Me on the Next World by Chris Manning

Maria is stuck in a rut. Bored with her life as an office drone, one day, she begins to see mysterious words appearing in the most unexpected places. Interpreting these words as instructions, she follows them to their thrilling conclusion: a life-changing event in which she pushes beyond the boundaries of herself and reality.

Staffed by Adam Rose

It isn't wise to steal from a wizard, even a retired one. That's what Grady Jameston finds out first-hand when he breaks into Eldryn Gnarlfelk's home, in an attempt to steal the wizard's staff. Will Grady make it through unscathed?

Jessie's Christmas Dreams by Katie Johns

Seven-year old Jessie is grounded, yet with the biggest imagination that brings anything to life, she discovers Dickensville, a Christmas Wonderland village. She makes a friend, Robbie, who is just as down on his luck, and the two adventure to seek Santa Claus, hoping he can help make things right for them. As Jessie gets older, she learns more about magical Dickensville and struggles with having a date to a middle school winter dance. Is her old friend an ideal candidate or is he too serious? An accident lands her there again the following year during a dramatic attempt to catch the attention of a high school crush. How does she physically and socially recover?

The Monster in My Dreams by Damian Stevenson

Tony Kreed lives a normal life, with the same schedule. However, out of the blue, Tony has a dream with a creature that makes no sense. He tries to solve his constant, nerve-wracking dreams, but no answers. In desperation, he goes insane, and stops at nothing to stop the dreams. Who would've guessed evil never stops at the mind, but at the soul?

The Girl Who Never Sleeps by Lorraine Bradner

Have you ever wanted to live two lives? That way you could experience more and get a do-over? Well, this young girl was able to experience that and more, but it wasn't normal. Instead of sleeping, she would switch between lives. A constant back and forth that was normal for Missy was abnormal for everyone else. Once it was discovered she had two lives, things took a turn for the worst. Join Missy as she navigates her two lives and explores why it is that she doesn't sleep or dream. You might just be surprised by what she finds out.

THE POND

The Pond is an exclusive body of water that offers magnificent healing powers for those who can afford to visit. One struggling family has faced hardship and saved to be able to visit The Pond, but is it truly everything that they thought it would be?

THE POND

By James Agee Jr.

THE POND

The harsh light illuminating the white walls is almost too much to look at. Floaters are visible in my eyesight, and I blink multiple times to try and clear them away with no success. The only visible detraction from the seas of white is the poster hanging behind the reception desk.

The employee working at the desk smiles relentlessly as I wonder at how they are able to work here each and every day without going blind. It occurs to me that if they were to go blind then they would probably be able to use their employee benefits to get a premium ticket to The Pond. I look at the other individuals sitting, waiting, for their chance to purchase a ticket. Perhaps they are here for themselves, or maybe they are like me, hoping to get a ticket for someone they love.

"Zola," the woman behind the desk calls out.

For a moment I am confused, looking around the room for the person whose name was just called, then I remember that my name is Zola. I have waited for this moment for so long that it hardly seems real. I stand and feel lightheaded, a sensation that is momentary. I have not eaten in the past twelve hours, choosing instead to save my credits and put them towards the ticket.

She motions for me to enter through the door to the right of her desk. I place my hand on the cool metal door and hear a slight noise as it reads my handprint, my Biocode, and confirms that I am indeed the person meant to be here. I would be worried had I not made this appointment weeks ago when I saw that I was nearing enough credits to be able to afford a ticket to The Pond. Anyone trying to purchase a ticket without the appropriate appointment scheduled will not get very far.

I open the door and a blast of sterile cool air hits me in the face.

"Go in." The woman at the desk urges me.

I take a few steps forward and hear the door shutting behind me. There is a clicking sound and I know without looking that the door will not budge if I were to attempt to go back. I find myself in a narrow hallway with only one way forward. The rumbling in my stomach distracts me for a moment before I remember why I am here and begin walking forward.

The hall opens onto a large room, the walls of which are gray, containing multiple booths that remind me of the ones I have seen in historical texts. They resemble what I know to be confession booths, only these are much sleeker with very few lines, and they are made of a metal material. I hear someone crying in one of the booths that has a red light blinking above it as I move towards one of the empty booths that has a green light indicating that it is not in use.

I step inside and have a seat upon the cold metal bench. A strand of hair falls from the astutely placed bun atop my head, and I brush it aside. One wall of the booth flashes and then comes to life with a video detailing what The Pond can offer. Everyone here knows what The Pond can do, that is why we are here, but I watch the video all the same.

"Your ticket to The Pond is your ticket to good health. Whatever disease or sickness bothers you will be gone upon entering the healing waters of The Pond." A calm voice says, filling the box with narration as the video shows footage of people entering the water in wheelchairs and running out of the waters with renewed bodies.

"Tickets to The Pond come in three distinguishable packages depending on your level of need."

I almost let out a small laugh. The packages have

nothing to do with need, none of this does. If tickets to The Pond were given based on need, then there would be no need to pay in obscene amounts of credits. The corporations that came together years ago and purchased the land where The Pond is located ensured that only those with the credits to afford a ticket would receive one.

"Package One is our lowest tier but still has many benefits. Not only will you receive admittance to The Pond which will heal you or your loved one of all ailments, but you will also receive follow-up counseling on how to live your new life. Learning to live without your ailments can be a difficult adjustment for some and a one-time counseling session via your in-home tele-screen will be your guide to living your best life."

I rolled my eyes, wishing for a way to skip over the next two packages as they are not something I can afford.

"Package Two includes everything from package one as well as our priority access line. This ensures that you have an expedited line experience when waiting for entrance to The Pond. After all, we know you are ready to be healed of your ailments and do not want to delay a moment longer.

Our last package, Package Three, includes everything from Packages One and Two as well as our concierge service. Skip the wait and go directly to The Pond. After leaving The Pond you will be presented with a membership card to our Pond Springs located around the Seven Lands, so anywhere you go you will have access to one of our healing sSprings for the rest of your long life.

It is time to decide how much you care about a healthy life and select the package that is right for you."

I let out a deep sigh that I did not even realize I had been holding in. A panel slides upwards and reveals the hand-pad, the greenish glow beckons me to place my hand upon it. I place my hand on the smooth glass and the screen displays all the credits in my account. The number is substantial for someone of my status, yet it seems so small in comparison to the thousands of hours it took me to obtain them.

"Please state aloud which package you wish to purchase." The voice says.

I look at the prices and how far away I am from package two., There is really only one option for people like me. I have worked my entire life to be able to afford a ticket to The Pond for my grandfather and I can only hope that my grandchildren will do the same for me. One ticket to The Pond will not afford an eternity of health like Package Three does, but it will provide another lifetime.

"Package One." I say begrudgingly.

"To confirm, you have selected Package One. Is that correct?"

"Yes."

I watch as the number of credits on the screen diminishes before my eyes. When the number stops decreasing, I am left with just enough credits to cover the rickshaw ride home. A thin metal card is dispensed from above and falls onto my lap. It seems like such a small thing for such a big price, but I know that this is my grandfather's only hope.

I exit the booth and am escorted out of the room by an attendant that appeared from seemingly nowhere. I am ushered down a set of stairs that lead directly to the ground floor where I exit and hail a rickshaw. I hold my palm to the driver's hand and transfer my remaining credits. They nod in approval, though I know they will not be happy to discover that I am unable to tip them at the end of the ride.

They drop me off at the tenement building where I live with my grandfather. We are on the lowest floor where there are no windows, not real ones anyway. Our tele-screen is set to display nature scenes around the clock so that we do not feel so confined in this space.

"You're back!" Grandpa says.

I look at him, his frail and skinny frame hardly able to stand up without support.

"I got it." I say.

He stands quiet for a moment before bringing his bony fingers to his eyes to wipe away tears.

"I told you not to spend all of your credits on me." He says guiltily.

"They were my credits to spend." I say as resolutely as I can manage while watching him cry.

He stumbles over to me and wraps me in a hug.

"You're the only one who cares about me." He informs me.

I don't have to say so, but I already know that it is the truth. I also know that he is the only person left who cares about me. Without him I would be all alone in what is left of this crazy world.

"When is it?" He asks.

I look at the thin piece of metal and see a date etched into it.

"This Saturmoor." I note.

"So soon?"

"Not soon enough."

He coughs and quickly pulls out his handkerchief. He holds it to his mouth and the white cloth quickly turns crimson with his blood.

"Not soon enough..." he manages after his coughing settles.

The next few days move at a crawl. Grandfather tries to stay positive, but I can see with each passing hour his energy is waning. I manage to scrounge up a few credits from doing odd jobs for the neighbors, enough to buy us a meal of salt skins. This is a meal that only the lowest of low in our society consume. There is no nutritional value, its only purpose to abate hunger for a brief period of time. I watched as the street-vendor scooped a small pile of animal skins into a pot of boiling grease and then place the skins into a bag before handing them over.

I pick a few hairs from the chunk of salt skin that I am holding before quicky chewing it. Grandpa takes his time chewing his boiled meal, trying to make it last. This is enough to hold us over until Saturmoor gets here. The nights are just as grueling as the days, as coughing fits plague him at every inopportune moment now this is when he takes most of his coughing fits. I try to put my pillow over my ears to block out the sounds of his pain because I know that there is nothing I can do to help him, but my pillow is so thin that it does not ever help.

The second sun rises in the pollution haze as the seventh moon begins to dip.

"Only a few more hours and you will be healed." I say, gently patting his shoulder and feeling nothing but bone.

He forces a smile as best as he can. I don't know that he could wait until the next Saturmoor, if he were not assigned this one then I dare not think what would happen. I would have tried to borrow some credits for a rickshaw to take us to The Pond, but the corporations that own The Pond are gracious enough to send a giga-bus around the city to collect those who have tickets and one of their relatives to transport them.

I worry that the closeness to everyone on the giga-bus will not be good for my grandpa, especially since almost everyone on the bus will be suffering from something themselves. We crowd onto the bus, and I implore a younger man to give up his seat for my grandpa, but he just turns his head and pretends not to hear me. Grandpa struggles to stand, especially when the giga-bus starts to move, but I do my best to hold him up.

I can feel the arm of the person beside of me. , wWe are all packed in here so closely that there is very little room to move. The air feels stale and smells of sickness. It never occurred to me until now that I might catch something from being on the bus, but there is no reason to worry about this because I never would have let Grandpa go to The Pond on his own.

Though I am somewhat curious about what The Pond looks like in person, I come with him out of a responsibility to see him through this. I cannot trust anyone else to get him there and I know that he is not strong enough to make it himself. The only reason they allow someone to tag along is to keep those on the brink of death from falling over before they get to The Pond.

I hold the metal ticket in my hand, clenching it so tightly that I create indentions in my skin that will be there for some time. Everything depends on this small ticket. The bus comes to a jarring stop and throws most everyone standing forward. The man who would not give up his seat jumps to his feet and pushes past the others so that he is the first one out the door.

I try to fight our way forward and carve out a path between the other bodies as they push and shove, but it is no use. We are some of the last ones to get off the bus. Grandpa is struggling to catch his breath and by the time he regains it enough to walk again, everyone else has gone ahead of us.

Amidst my worrying about Grandpa, I notice the fresh scent of The Pond and know that we have truly arrived. There is an expansive gate that warns of shocking anyone that attempts to get too close to it and guards posted every few feet. There is a long line forming near an angular structure.

"We best hurry." Grandpa says.

I can tell that he is struggling to breathe. Today will be his last day unless we get him to the waters soon. We get in line and are quickly asked for our ticket. The person checking the tickets asks tersely for everyone who will be visiting The Pond to present their ticket. When it is our turn I hand over the ticket and wait for them to hand it back after confirming that we are where we are supposed to be.

"You're in the wrong line." They inform us.

My heart sinks, I do not want to waste time switching lines when we are so close to having Grandpa healed. They point to a line that is so far from the structure that I had not even noticed it before.

"That can't be!. How long does that line usually take?." I ask pleadingly.

"If it moves fast then you should be able to get in The Pond in about twelve hours."

"We don't have twelve hours! Look at him! , hHe can hardly breathe!."

They look at Grandpa for a moment and then shrug their shoulders, "The more time you waste talking to me, the further back in line you'll be. I suggest you go now."

We take their advice, though we have no other choice, and switch lines. Our new line is at the edges of the property and the structure looks so very far away. The suns and moons in the sky move drastically by the time that we near the halfway point of the line. An elderly couple in front of us collapse from exhaustion and nobody stops to help them., Tthe line just keeps moving around their motionless bodies.

There is such a careless atmosphere here that I worry nobody would care if the same happened to us. Others seem to have thought to bring various food items with them to sustain them throughout their long waits. We would not have had enough credits to afford any food to bring with us even if I had thought about that.

I do my best to stay positive and not think about the fact that Grandpa is barely hanging on at this point.

"We're getting closer!"

He nods, not strong enough to manage any words.

A few stray tears roll from my eyes, and I turn my head to wipe them away, not wanting him to see me cry. This should be a happy occasion, one that I have worked hard to accomplish. The weight of the metal card feels lighter and lighter as we continue to stand in our spots. Suddenly the worry of what might happen if we don't make it in time infiltrates my thoughts.

"I don't think I can stand much longer." Grandpa manages in a weak voice.

"Just a little longer. We're almost there." I encourage him.

A woman in front of us turns around and looks pityingly upon Grandpa and me.

"I'd offer you a bite of my bread but...you know how many credits things cost." She says to me.

I honestly believe that she feels sorry for us, but she does not feel sorry enough to give us any of her bread. I nod and she turns away eating the last few bites of her food. Without credits it is impossible to survive, the corporations saw to that many years ago.

Against all odds, Grandpa holds on until we are only a few people away from the structure.

"We are so close!" I say to him.

I can see now that the structure is nothing more than a glorified entrance. We step through the entrance and are asked for our ticket once more. This time the attendant keeps it and does not give it back.

"Which one of you will be going into The Pond?" They ask.

"He is." I say motioning to Grandpa.

"He may proceed forward; you can stand on the veranda and watch." We are instructed.

I am escorted to an overlook that appears to be made of a strong glass material where I am told to wait until after he enters and exits The Pond. The scent of the pond emanates everywhere and the crystalline glow of the waters appears inviting. A thin layer of mist rolls over the waters as I see people bobbing in and out of the waters. They go in slowly and with painstaking effort and emerge with vigor.

I cannot wait to see the same happen to Grandpa. I look over the edge of the railing and see that an attendant is also with him. He cranes his neck and looks up to me. I smile down to him, but the look on his face frightens me, it is pleading and filled with a lifetime of sadness.

As the smile slips from my face, so does Grandpa slip from the grip of the attendant. Meer feet from the lapping edge of The Pond Grandpa lays motionless on the ground. I let out a guttural scream as I watch the attendant reach down and check for a pulse. They shake their head "no" and call the other attendants to help carry away the body...his body.

I fall to the translucent floor and weep as I feel the loss of the only person in the world who cared about me. I do not cry for the thousands of hours of hard labor that have been wasted to purchase the ticket, for what I had purchased was nothing more than hope. Hope is such a volatile thing that I should have known better than to assume it would realize itself in my life.

I cry for what feels like an hour before someone arrives to escort me back to the giga-bus. I do not ask if I can use the ticket instead, the thought does not even cross my mind until much later. I consider it a loss, but the greater loss of my grandpa is one that I know I will feel the effects of for the rest of my life. The attendant had offered to send the body back to our address or provide a pond-side burial free of charge. Since I have no credits to bury him, I had to accept their offer.

The next days of my life pass in a blur. I do not worry

about food, but one of our neighbors stopped by with a bag of salt skins and molded cheese to pay their respects and that has sustained me. I thanked them but did not invite them in, there would be no point as the inside of our apartment is the same as all the others.

I stand by the tele-screen and watch as the wild creatures move about the grassy lands, a place that I will never actually see in real life, and I wonder at how I will go on. A large mammal passes by and takes a drink from the digital pond before me, nothing like The Pond. A pain in my chest rises and though I unconsciously try and fight it back but I cannot. I cough and look at the screen before me where a splash of red begins to drip.

ABOUT JAMES AGEE JR.

James Agee Jr. is the author of multiple young adult and children's novels. His books offer a variety of stories so that all readers are able to find one of his works to can enjoy.

MEET ME ON THE NEXT WORLD

Maria is stuck in a rut. Bored with her life as an office drone, one day, she begins to see mysterious words appearing in the most unexpected places. Interpreting these words as instructions, she follows them to their thrilling conclusion: a life-changing event in which she pushes beyond the boundaries of herself and reality.

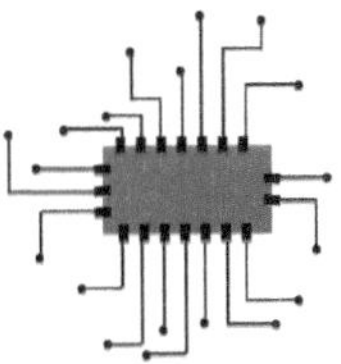

MEET ME ON THE NEXT WORLD

By Chris Manning

MEET ME ON THE NEXT WORLD

With her mug planted firmly beneath the coffee machine, Maria pushed the button, only to hear that familiar, loathsome gurgling sound. She heaved an exasperated sigh as the last few drops from the carafe trickled into her mug. *Out of coffee,* she thought. *It's going to be one of those Mondays.*

Under harsh, fluorescent lights, she shuffled to her cubicle, which was surrounded by dozens of other cubicles. They were all occupied by workers dressed in the same outfits, which were more like uniforms: blouses, pencil skirts, and high heels for the women; , collared shirts, slacks, and loafers for the men.

Feeling hungover (after too many glasses of wine the previous night), she threw her purse on her desk and sank into her swivel chair. She turned on her computer, and as it booted up, she stared at her keyboard, lamenting her circumstances in life. She was single, with no prospects of a relationship, and stuck in a dead-end job as a customer service rep for a company named Safe Insurance. She hated that name.

Every day's the same, she thought. *I wake up, drive my red Toyota Celica to work (always the same route), and enter the same garage where I park in the same spot (C96 on the 5th floor). Then I take the elevator to the 8th floor of this dreary office building. Day in and day out... The only variable is the coffeemaker. Will there or won't there be coffee left? Even my thoughts are routine. I'm pretty sure I thought about this yesterday... I'm young, intelligent, and fairly attractive. What the hell happened? I know what happened. Nothing. I took this job straight out of college, never bothered to look for anything else, never even traveled, and so this is what I get. Is 33 too young to be having a midlife crisis?*

She ran her hands through her chestnut-colored hair, folded her arms, and leaned back in her chair so that she was staring straight up at the ceiling. *Probably full of asbestos,* she thought. This was terrible. It wasn't even 9 am, and she was already sinking into a pit of despair. She needed a distraction.

She resolved to play a game of connect-the-dots by looking for pictures in the ceiling, which was made of fiberboard and perforated with tiny black dots. Cheryl, her mousy neighbor in the next cubicle, was staring at her with curiosity. Maria was too busy to care as she gazed at the ceiling. *Oh, look! I think I see a sailboat! No, wait! It's a castle! Oh god, I'm bored...*

And then, she noticed something that gave her pause. She sat up and squinted her eyes. She could see that something was written on the ceiling tile directly above her, as if someone had arranged those tiny dots into small letters.

Unable to read it, she stood up, stretched her neck, and strained her eyes. She still couldn't make it out. This was too much for her to just let go, so she kicked off her heels, climbed onto her desk, and stood on her tiptoes.

There! Now she could read it:

C L I M B

That was it. Nothing else. Just "CLIMB." She looked down at her desk and then at the word again. *Why would someone write the word "CLIMB" onto the ceiling? What could that mean? Was someone playing a joke on her? Were they just trying to get me to climb onto my desk? Are they laughing at me right now?*

Maria glanced down at Cheryl, who quickly turned

back to her computer. From this height, Cheryl looked like she was a million miles away. Maria climbed down, not even noticing the strange stares she was receiving from her co-workers.

She asked Cheryl what she thought it could mean. Already annoyed by Maria's odd behavior, Cheryl told her that she couldn't see anything but a bunch of random black dots.

"Even if there is a word in all that jumble, it was probably written when this office was being built. Probably put there by some bored construction worker."

"You're probably right," Maria replied, still staring at the word. "But why write 'CLIMB'? The person must have had a very odd sense of humor."

Cheryl just shrugged and walked to the break-room, hoping someone had made more coffee.

Throughout the rest of the day, Maria sat in her cubicle, leaning back in her chair, her hands clasped behind her head, gazing up at the ceiling. The word "CLIMB" seemed to scream at her. She could think of nothing else, as though she was being drawn to it like an invisible tractor beam.

She pondered all the possible meanings, turning the word over in her mind: *"CLIMB." It was such an ordinary word (dull, actually). But at the same time, it was full of possibilities. Was it meant to be taken literally or figuratively?*

To keep her mind on her work, she forced herself to keep her eyes on her monitor. It didn't work. "CLIMB" hovered over her cubicle and seemed to follow her wherever she went. She ended up googling all the definitions and interpretations of the word. Ultimately, she decided to interpret it literally. Thinking about it in the figurative sense was too problematic...too ambiguous.

With her attention a million miles away, she didn't notice the phone ringing off the hook or her manager, Richard, giving her dirty looks as he passed by her cubicle. She even missed an important meeting, not that she'd have been able to pay attention anyway.

"...you just seem to be in another world," Richard said as he stood over her, sipping his cup of coffee. "...and part of our job is responding to our customers in a timely manner."

Staring at the ceiling, his voice drifted in and out of her consciousness. She knew she better say something, so she made up some paltry excuse about personal problems at home. He nodded slowly and glanced at her as he walked away. He was a nice enough boss and Maria knew he'd always had a thing for her. The other women in her department probably would have jumped at the chance to go out with him, but Maria never saw herself as the type of woman who dated her boss, or anyone for that matter.

It just all seemed so predictable, so ordinary. She could already see her life play out like one of those old film reels: First the job, then the dating, then the marriage, then the kids... Perhaps that was her problem. She just didn't "fit."

Regardless, normally, after being called out for neglecting her duties, she would have gone home and replayed the event in her head a million times. After all, she needed a job. But, strangely, for the first time in her life, it didn't matter to her. She'd stumbled upon an obscure clue to an even more obscure mystery—one she was determined to solve.

When Maria got home that night, instead of walking into her little bungalow guesthouse (which she rented from an elderly woman) she went straight to the garage, found a ladder, and propped it against the side of the house. She kicked off her heels again, and as she took her first tentative steps up, the word "CLIMB" ran through the back of her mind.

Within a minute, she'd reached the top. It was exactly what one would expect—a slightly sloped, shingled rooftop. She found a comfortable spot and sat down, holding her legs with her arms. She gazed at the horizon and the surrounding houses below. As dusk settled over the neighborhood, lights began to appear in the windows of the houses.

She wondered what people were doing at this hour. Eating dinner, conversing, watching TV, and enjoying time with their loved ones. It sounded nice, but deep inside, she knew that life wasn't for her. Ever since she was a girl, she knew she was searching for something more...she just didn't know what "more" was. And, as painful as it was to admit, even if she did know, she'd probably be too afraid to go after it.

She sat a moment longer, enjoying the cool evening breeze, before noticing a grimy coffee can in the corner of the roof. It was full to the brim with butts and half-finished cigarettes.

I guess I'm not the first one to come up here. Taking careful steps, she climbed over and picked it up. *I suppose if I don't empty this, no one will. I'll empty it and put it back up here. That way, the next lonely person who climbs up here will already have an ashtray waiting for them (assuming they smoke).*

As she climbed back down the ladder, she made it a point to forget this nonsense once and for all. After all, there was safety in routine, in conformity; she just had to accept it.

But just as she reached the bottom, she slipped on the bottom rung and dropped the can, spilling the cigarettes all over the ground. She quietly cursed to herself and leaned down to sweep them up in her hand. And then, peering closer, she saw it: As if hidden in plain sight, some of the half-finished cigarettes formed a word:

HIGHER

She felt like she was staring through a portal to another world, one in which anything was possible. But just as she registered the impossible odds of this happening, a strong gust of wind scattered the cigarettes. "No!" she yelled in frustration. "You've got to be kidding me!" If only she'd had her phone, maybe she could have recorded it or taken a picture. But then who would believe me?

She shivered, glanced around self-consciously, and hurried into her house. Instead of heating a microwave dinner and turning on the TV as she normally did, she popped a couple of Tylenol PMs and went straight to bed. Lying in bed, she stared up at the ceiling, lost in thought. *Climb...higher...climb higher...* She turned on her side and closed her eyes until she drifted off to sleep.

The next day, although Maria knew it made no sense, she made a point to observe every minute detail around her. She honmed in on the smallest things: the Cheerios floating in her cereal bowl, the track marks on freshly mowed lawns, the cracks in the sidewalks. On her way to work, she stopped at a newspaper stand and flipped through every newspaper and magazine on the rack, waiting for another piece of the puzzle to jump out. The owner glared at this strange woman and wondered if he should call the police. Once she looked up and saw his expression, she slowly slunk away.

After parking in her usual spot on the 5th floor of the garage, she rode the elevator to the 8th floor of her office building, walked to her cubicle, climbed onto her desk, and inspected the ceiling. Nothing! She couldn't even make out the word "CLIMB" anymore.

Finally, she marched past Cheryl's cubicle (who gave her a hostile look), and with folded arms, stood and stared out the large window. After about 20 minutes, Richard walked up to her and lightly tapped her on the shoulder.

"Hey there, Maria. There are a lot of customers on hold. Is there a reason why you're not at your desk?"

"I'm waiting for a sign, Richard!"

"A sign? From whom...? If you don't mind my asking."

I have *no* idea! It's so frustrating! But that's not the worst part. I don't even know what they're trying to tell me!"

An awkward silence followed before Richard spoke again.

"Okay...why don't you take the rest of the day off..."

"That's a good idea. I need some time to think this over."

When Maria turned around to leave, she realized a small crowd of her coworkers was standing behind them, whispering to one another. With her head down, she strode past them and into the elevator.

But instead of taking it to the lobby, she rode up to the 12th floor, which was as high as employees were allowed. From there, she managed to convince the security guard that she was a site inspector and that she needed to take the elevator to the rooftop for an inspection (unescorted, of course).

"Here I am! I'm climbing higher!" she shouted as she rode the service elevator to the roof. "Climb higher...any higher and I'd be climbing Mount Everest!"

She smiled with amusement. "Maybe I'm being stalked. Maybe it's a psychotic personal trainer...or maybe a motivational speaker trying to spread the gospel."

Her smile quickly faded as she realized what she was doing. She hadn't committed any crimes yet (although lying to a security guard could be considered a fireable offense), but she was talking to herself and riding up this elevator—following clues that only she could see. Even she could see that this was crazy.

As she walked out of the elevator, she couldn't help feeling disappointed when all she saw was a flat, ordinary rooftop with only a couple of HVAC units and a small transmission antenna--typical fixtures (typically found on the roofs of office buildings).

She gazed over the edge at the adjacent buildings and then across the street at the towering monolithic parking structure where she parked every day. Thin, white sheets of clouds hovered over it like flying saucers.

She walked over to the rooftop antenna and examined the skinny rods. *Could* they *be trying to communicate with me? Aliens...?* She froze and immediately pushed this thought from her mind. *This is what crazy people do,* she thought. *They find something meaningless in their lives and convince themselves it means something...that they're somehow special. AND I AM NOT CRAZY!*

She turned around and walked back to the elevator where she would take it to the 8th floor, apologize to Richard and quietly return to her cubicle. And this time, she really would forget this nonsense. She was halfway to the elevator before she froze in her tracks. She spun around, and with her mouth agape, stared up at the parking structure again, which now seemed to loom over her like a gothic cathedral. The clouds just above it, their shapes now full and majestic, spelled out the word:

FURTHER

Shielding her eyes from the sun, she gazed at the word, frightened but exhilarated. She knew that there could be a million reasons why this word appeared in the sky. This could be the result of a plane skywriting a message, an advertisement, or a personal message to someone else...this could be completely unrelated to her. Maybe it wasn't even there. Regardless, this time, she was determined to get a picture for evidence. She reached into her pocket to pull out her phone, but when she looked back up, the clouds had dissipated, the word no longer there. She slowly nodded, and with a blank expression, sat down and stared up at the sky. She sat there for hours...waiting.

As the evening set in, she laid down on the roof, staring at the stars in the night sky. Surely, the stars, just like which people had been contemplating for centuries, would tell her more. But she didn't see anything, no unusual patterns, not even a constellation. Finally, she took the elevator back down and drove home in a daze, wondering if she was, indeed, losing her mind.

Maria woke up an hour late the next morning. She'd had trouble sleeping due to unsettling dreams in which she was falling endlessly down a black hole. As she plunged down the abyss, she could perceive a light emanating from below. Her gut reaction was that this was some fiery pit she was approaching, but as she got closer, instead of the harsh red of a blazing fire, the light took on a warm, white glow. It seemed to welcome her. Even as she hurtled towards it, she no longer felt afraid. Just as the light enveloped her completely, she woke up, staring at the morning sunlight peeking through her blinds.

She crawled out of bed, put on her Ziggy Stardust t-shirt (which she hadn't worn since her 20s) and blue jeans, and left for work that morning. Before she left, she listened to the last of the three messages Richard had left for her about her recent behavior and how they would have to "have a talk" when she got in.

As she drove up the spiral ramp of the parking garage where she worked, she was about to get off on the 5th floor where she always parked in C96. Only this time, she kept driving...further. *Why not?* she thought. *I'm going to be fired, so what difference does it make if I'm late?*

It was an odd sensation as she couldn't remember if she'd ever driven past the 5th floor. "Climb...higher... further..." she whispered as slowly pressed down on the gas pedal, now speeding up as she drove up and around the 6th, 7th, and 8th floors.

If she'd told anyone why she was doing this, they'd either look at her with fear or pity in their eyes (or both). Either way, she couldn't care less.

Suddenly, the speedometer on her dashboard panel began to flutter wildly, displaying strange symbols instead of the usual numbers. Leaning closer, she watched it eventually settle on a word that was clear and unmistakable:

FASTER

THIS TIME, she floored the gas pedal, and the tires screeched in response. As she careened up each floor, flying around each curve like a Formula 1 driver, instead of tensing up, the muscles in her shoulders felt lighter, like a great weight had been lifted.

Accelerating faster and faster up the spiral ramp, like a merry-go-round gone haywire, she soon became dizzy and began to...giggle. Starting small, chuckling here and there, it soon evolved into full-blown, gut-busting laughter. Like a child spinning in circles, she was doing something that made no sense whatsoever, and she'd never felt better in her life.

"Climb...higher...further...faster...sounds like a goddamn car commercial!" she shouted. "What are you? Some demented car salesman?!" She laughed so hard, that tears filled her eyes. Her mind reeled at this sudden turn of events, and she wasn't sure how much more she could take before she completely broke down.

As she passed the 16th floor, her foot still firmly planted on the gas, whizzing past a series of concrete columns, she realized she hadn't seen any other cars for a while. She was all alone up here. *Well, I've been alone my whole life,* she thought. *What else is new?* This sent her into another fit of laughter. "Up, up, and away!" she shouted with elation, as she hurtled to the 20th floor.

Her car began to rattle and shake, and as it twisted around a narrow curve, it skidded and slammed into the side of a concrete wall, shooting sparks into the air. "Whoops! That's not good!" she said between bouts of laughter. "Oh well! Buy the ticket, take the ride!"

Twisting the wheel, the weight of the car pulled her this way and that so that she was now scraping the walls of the garage at every turn. In the darkness, the car spiraled up the ramps like a spinning firework. Yet, she somehow managed to keep up the exquisite speed, as though the momentum itself was propelling her up and around every turn.

The concrete girders hanging above her were now blurring together like a series of still frames in a flip book. Now, on the 25th floor, she looked out over the side of the parking garage.

Where she expected to see the familiar sight of office buildings, she saw only blue sky and sunshine.

I must be really high up! she thought. *I didn't think there were that many floors in this garage...Guess I'll just have to keep going 'till I hit the top.*

Just as she was about to turn onto the 30th floor, she suddenly glimpsed sunlight up ahead. *And here we are... the rooftop, at last,* she thought. She let out a heavy sigh and eased her foot off the gas. *I suppose even this ride had to eventually come to an —*

But before she could finish her thought, the Toyota lurched forward, as if someone had taken control of the car and was now flooring the gas pedal. Her eyes darted in every direction as she felt her sanity being stretched to its breaking point.

Her last rational thought, as she roared up the ramp leading onto the roof, was that the ground would soon level out and she'd be able to jump out of the car. She'd be injured, perhaps badly, but at least she wouldn't collide into a wall or worse, drive off the roof and careen head-long to the ground below. Then again, maybe that's how this was all meant to end. She took a deep breath.

Then, to her utter amazement, just as she emerged onto the roof, sunlight poured through the windshield, and her little Toyota, which she used to drive to work every day for as long as she could remember, shot upwards, rocketing towards the sun like Icarus himself.

Maria screamed in wide-eyed terror as she gripped the steering wheel, now using it to hang on for dear life. Soaring upwards, through blue sky and white clouds, she could feel a sinking feeling in her stomach and thought she might throw up. And, yet, she managed to keep herself together, emitting only an occasional whimper as she witnessed the world below growing smaller by the second.

Higher and higher she flew. She squeezed her eyes shut, praying that this vivid nightmare would come to an end. But when she opened them again, instead of waking to the sound of her alarm clock, all she could perceive was the sound of intense wind buffeting her car, deep blue sky, and warm sunlight bathing her face and arms.

She was able to gather her senses long enough to glance back at the earth below. She was already so high above the ground, that the buildings and cars below resembled toys.

She turned back around, where she was once again greeted by blue sky. *The folks at home are never going to believe this!* she thought, a wild look in her eyes.

After being briefly enveloped in whiteness, the Toyota blasted through a blanket of white clouds like a cork shot from a wine bottle.

Now beaten and mangled, the car looked more like a hunk of red and black scrap metal than a functioning automobile. Maria knew she didn't have much longer. "Okay, this has been fun, but whoever's doing this...you can stop now! I don't want to die!" she cried hysterically.

The windshield began to split in myriad places. Before long, it turned into an extravagant web of fissures spread out before her. With all her strength, Maria pulled herself forward so that she could read the word spelled out by the cracks:

RELAX

Within seconds, the windshield shattered and blew outward, flying off the car like a bird released into the wild by its master. Icy wind blasted Maria's face, blowing her hair and t-shirt into a frenzy.

Before she could process what was happening, the car, crumbled to pieces around her. One by one, twisted chunks of metal tumbled back to earth like jettisoned rubbish.

Somehow, incredibly, Maria was unharmed; not a single scratch on her. Like a phoenix rising from the flames, she continued to soar upwards, propelled by a force beyond human understanding.

Every part of her rational being urged her, begged her, to scream, to cry out in sheer panic. Instead, up here with nothing but blue sky, white clouds, and the wind whistling in her ears, she felt a sense of exhilaration and... calm. She somehow knew she was intimately connected to *whoever* or *whatever* had been sending her these messages. This had all been planned, as if her whole life had been building up to this moment. No harm would come to her. All she had to do was...let go...relax.

As she continued her upward trajectory, she stopped flailing her arms and, instead, let them fall to her side. She discovered that she was not only still ascending, but that she was picking up speed. She suddenly heard an enormous boom all around her as she broke the sound barrier. It wouldn't be long before she was traveling faster than the speed of light.

She stared at her hands and arms. Her flesh began to char and blister from the intense heat being generated by her speed. Her clothes and hair suddenly erupted into flames. But, still, she felt no pain, only a warm glow permeating her being. She laughed as she imagined what she must look like at this point: a blackened corpse within a ball of fire, hurtling towards the upper atmosphere.

Gazing up at the darkening sky, the last thing Maria saw before she broke earth's gravity and entered the blackness of space, was her body disintegrating into thin air—beginning with her legs, then her torso, and finally her head. There was no pain or fear as she observed the particles of matter dancing away from her physical self.

Now as pure energy and consciousness, the last words Maria heard (*sensed*) before she shed the vestiges of her previous life floated through her like a gentle breeze. She heard her own voice, finally breaking through the noise and chaos of reality:

Maria, by taking these first steps, you have found me as you have found yourself. You no longer need to search for me...for you are me...as I am you.

As Maria's consciousness entered the starry vacuum of space, she was filled with awe and excitement. She wondered what it would be like to meet her future self and to explore all the marvelous possibilities the universe offered. Racing through a kaleidoscopic array of stars, nebulas, and galaxies, she knew her life would never be the same again.

ABOUT CHRIS MANNING

Chris Manning was born and raised in Santa Cruz, CA before moving to San Francisco and eventually Los Angeles. He writes short speculative Fiction and feature news articles.

STAFFED

It isn't wise to steal from a wizard, even a retired one.
That's what Grady Jameston finds out first-hand when he
breaks into Eldryn Gnarlfelk's home, in an attempt to
steal the wizard's staff. Will Grady make it through
unscathed?

STAFFED

By Adam Rose

STAFFED

The staff was a rather unassuming piece of woodcraft. It was a straight length of ash about five and a half feet in length and completely unadorned, save for the patterns of the wood itself. It bore no etchings, carvings, or wood burnings. It appeared to be nothing more than a mundane walking stick, which in truth, was the only purpose it served these days. However, only a dullard would think it such.

This seemingly unostentatious rod was the Staff of Eldryn Gnarlfelk, one of the last Master Wizards to walk the world. It was with this staff that Eldryn had brought down the fire of the stars themselves on the army of the vile and fetid Lord Oudhaus. It was with this staff that he bound and entombed the powerful demon Bedreil. It was with this staff that he cast the curses that had forced the tyrannical ruler of the land to give in to his people's cries for democracy.

That was all in the past, though. Now, Eldryn had retired, taking his place in history and legend, leaving magic to the charlatans and petty conjurers of the current era. He hadn't used magic such as that in centuries. Make no mistake, though, both wizard and staff retained as much power as ever. Staff, wizard, and the home in which the two resided was well- protected, as one would expect a wizard's home to be. Only a fool would dare sneak in under the cover of night and steal the fabled Staff.

However, oOne such fool was Grady Jameston, and he dared. Grady was dared by his friends, who wished him to prove his mettle, to slip into the ancient wizard's home and steal his staff. For, you see, young, foolhardy Grady didn't believe in magic., Hhe didn't believe that the walking stick was anything more than that, and he certainly didn't believe Old Man Gnarlfelk was a wizard. Thus, he took the dare, slipping in through a window. What he failed to notice was that his friends left as soon as he entered the house.

Upon entering the dwelling, he found nothing odd. It appeared to be nothing more than the home of an old bachelor. Grady looked to his left and saw the kitchen with a sink and stove and a dining room with a large table. To his right, he saw the stairs leading to the second level.

(He heard snoring coming from that direction.) Before him was a large, comfortable-looking chair which sat in front of the fireplace. The fire had been banked for the night, its red glow giving an eerie appearance to the life-size wolf statues on either side of the fireplace and the mounted eagle above the mantle. The staff sat in the corner by the fireplace.

Grady walked over to it and grabbed it. As soon as he did, the staff flashed with an electric blue light. An ominous wind howled down the chimney, blowing out the fire. The boy thought nothing of the wind and seemed not to notice the blue light. As he passed again in front of the fireplace, the fire reignited into an amethyst inferno. A face appeared in the flames.

"Who dares steal from this house?" it roared. Grady was frozen with fear. The eyes of the fiery face looked directly into his and he said, **"Sic him!."**

The eyes of the wolves and the eagle glowed amber. The stone on the wolf statues cracked as the beasts came to life, shaking themselves, sending bits of stone flying. They began to stalk towards the boy. The eagle lifted off its perch and flew his head. Grady ducked just in time. As he turned to run, he caught sight of the flaming, violet face flying out of the fireplace, trailing purple fire.

Grady ran for his life, but the door seemed to be getting further away. Thrice more he had to duck the eagle's claws. Finally, he reached the door, only to find it locked . In desperation, he pointed the staff at the door and cried, "Open." Surprisingly, it worked.

Grady made a dash for the hedge that surrounded Gnarlfelk's home. The hedge vined out and wrapped up the boy, pulling him to it and holding him fast, forcing him to release the staff. The wolves came within a foot of him and stood there, growling and , baying at him. The eagle swooped down and picked up the staff.

The floating, fiery, purple face slammed into the ground and resolved itself into Old Man Gnarlfelk. The eagle dropped the staff into his outstretched hand, circled, and landed on his shoulder. The old wizard walked towards the trapped boy.

"Ah, Grady Jameston," the wizard said, "The only young fool who would have the audacity to attempt something such as this, the only fool in the village who doesn't believe in magic, the only fool stupid enough to steal from a wizard. You didn't believe in my power, and you tried to steal my staff. Now you shall feel my wrath!"

Old Man Gnarlfelk stepped back and pointed his staff at Grady. He incanted, *"Trechaxis, mortantum, veloco, amirtrum!"*

Grady dissolved. It was an odd sensation, feeling like dust being blown on the wind. He reformed in an enormous stone chamber that appeared to be underground. The room was lit by torches on the wall and a roaring fire pit in the center of the floor. Glowing red and gold sigils ran over the walls, ceiling, and floor. One corner of the room was shrouded in darkness, out of which stared two glowing, red, football-sized eyes. As the owner of the eyes stood, Grady heard the rattle of chains. Something stepped into the firelight.

The creature was fifteen feet tall and had skin the color of coal. Its entire body was heavily muscled. Its fingers ended in claws, and its feet were cloven hooves. Ram's horns curled from the top of its head, down, around, and behind its pointed ears, and wicked, white, dagger-like teeth gleamed in its mouth. It wore only a loin-cloth. Silver manacles affixed to the wall circled its neck, wrists, and ankles, and that emanated a golden light encir-cled its neck, wrists, and ankles. These were attached to chains, which emanated a matching light, affixed to the wall.

"W-w-w-what a-a-are y-y-y-you?" Grady whimpered. When the creature spoke, its voice was gruff, hollow, and ancient.

"I am Bedreil," the creature replied. Its voice was gruff, hollow, and ancient.

Grady nearly screamed. He had heard stories of how Eldryn Gnarlfelk had supposedly imprisoned this powerful demon, but thought that they were just that, stories. The demon spoke again.

"That wretched wizard, Eldryn Gnarlfelk, imprisoned me here nearly a millennium ago. He left me alone, bored, and...*hungry*. Now, after all this time, it seems he has been kind enough to send me a...hmm hmm hmm...*snack*."

The demon cackled wildly. The boy *did* scream as one of the clawed hands grasped him and pulled him toward those wicked dagger-teeth.

ABOUT ADAM ROSE

Adam Rose is a middle school English teacher and lover of all things fantasy. This is his first time being published.

JESSIE'S CHRISTMAS DREAMS

Seven-year old Jessie is grounded, yet with the biggest imagination that brings anything to life, she discovers Dickensville, a Christmas Wonderland village. She makes a friend, Robbie, who is just as down on his luck, and the two adventure to seek Santa Claus, hoping he can help make things right for them. As Jessie gets older, she learns more about magical Dickensville and struggles with having a date to a middle school winter dance. Is her old friend an ideal candidate or is he too serious? An accident lands her there again the following year during a dramatic attempt to catch the attention of a high school crush. How does she physically and socially recover?

JESSIE'S CHRISTMAS DREAMS

By Katie Johns

Jessie was in more trouble than a seven-year-old should be in, and some of it wasn't even her fault. She had the biggest imagination that she fed with making art and writing stories every chance she got. And her imagination just wouldn't let her focus on much else. For a few weeks, she had been up past her bedtime, doodling and writing her own stories, anything but homework and studying. As a result, she received low grades on some assignments and tests. a few weeks prior. Sure, she should have been studying and doing homework instead of doodling and writing her own stories. Beyond that, she had done anything but homework past her bedtime. She had the biggest imagination that she fed with making art and writing stories every chance she got. And her imagination just wouldn't let her focus on much else. In turn, hHer lack of sleep also made morning routines and behaving at school tougher. She even tried to lie about a few questionable instances, both to her teacher and her parents. The tipping point though was when the classroom bully ruined her art project. The indifferent substitute in class that day wrote her up for Jessie's reactionary outburst, seeming to ignore what incited it.

For the first time in Jessie's life, she received detention and her parents grounded her. She had to sit in for recess one day, and at the end of the day for a whole month, she only went between home and school for a month. She was not allowed to watch tv for that long either. Her grounding would be extended one more day for every night she was caught sneaking a book or journal after bedtime, and her parents were on the dot when checking on her. She did her homework at the dining room table, studied with her parents, and she could only use the computer or her art supplies if an assignment needed it. The strict discipline improved her sleep, behavior, and grades, but confined her hungry imagination. And with how close this all was to Christmas, she worried about whether she'd get the gift she'd been dying for, or if she'd be able to enjoy it. She wanted the Ultimate Drawing Box, an expensive kit that included neon, pastel, and glitter pens, glittery markers, watercolors, sketchpads, and color-in stickers.

Jessie's parents had to go out of town for a weekend while she was still grounded. So, she was sent to her grandparents' house, a country hilltop acre thirty miles away. Something about her grandparents' place could satiate her imaginative appetite more than her devices at home often could. Nearly everything she saw had a life of its own, from her grandmother's collectible figurines to the photos and albums of her mother and uncles when they were younger, to the vast, treed lot surrounding the house. She was easily an adventurer in uncharted territory or an explorer running from danger when she played outside there.

Also, she couldn't be stopped from helping her grandparents decorate for Christmas. She was helping them after all. She couldn't be as well-behaved if she didn't and it wasn't necessarily any of her own art material she was actively using. The tree went up, wreaths, bows, and electric window candles came out, and so did Grandmother's ceramic Christmas village collection, the matriarch thinking her granddaughter who also thought she was old enough to be careful with it now. Together, they cleaned off some shelf space for it and laid a cotton sheet across it. Next, the buildings were unboxed and arranged, followed by the tiny people and a few animals. Finally, the cords were collected and connected to a plug, adding to the display the final touch of a warm glow. Fewer things gave

Jessie her more wonder, and her imagination felt free again! Carefully rearranging the characters and developing their daily lives, She played with it until she fell asleep, carefully rearranging the characters and developing their intricate daily lives..

When she woke the next morning, everything outside was white! A good six inches of snow fell overnight with more to come throughout the day. She couldn't wait to get out and play in it! Once suited and booted, she hopped out to the yard, amused by how deep her feet sank into the snow. First, she made snow angels for her wintry haven. Lumbering to her feet, she twirled in circles with her face to the sky and tongue out to catch snowflakes. She laughed while watching a draft blow snow off the house, carrying towards where she called the eastern woods--or just the right side of the property from the backyard. She felt a need to follow it.

Her only limits today were the tree-marked property lines distinguishing her grandparents' property from the neighbors', the road above the front yard, and the thick shrub line along the edge of the backyard. Jessie would turn right around when she knew she was near them; anyone watching her would just see a little girl running sprints and circles over her own tracks, but in her mind, every turn often led someplace new. More snow swirled from the building and the trees as she reached the entrance edge of the wood. She weaved through the trees, still trying to chase the snowy wind.

Several rounds and paces into her adventure, all the familiar landmarks of her grandparents' property disappeared: the gray storage shed, the detached garage, the gravel driveway. All Jessie could see in any direction were snow and trees for miles. The snow on the ground dusted over her earlier tracks and climbed further up her boots, making her feel smaller. She looked up to the sky, wondering if she could determine east from west, but the view was as covered and colorless as anywhere else. Jessie imagined this is what living in a snow-globe might be like. She determined to keep a straighter path from that point, thinking she'd reach the other end before too long if nobody shook it too hard.

She trudged on several more miles, still not encountering the opposite side of any snow globe interior. Or much less any distinct sign of civilization for that matter. She learned about history and geography in school now-- new topics which also sparked her imagination--had she possibly imagined herself back in time before people lived where her grandparents did? If so, she realized that people might not even start living where she was for at least a hundred years! Historical times without all the people and places was less interesting than she pretended it to be.

Remembering the lessons on the different kinds of climates, Jessie decided she couldn't be at her grandparents' anymore. They lived in a temperate region; with this much snow, she had to be in a polar one at best. Way up north...the North Pole perhaps! Maybe she should be looking for elves and reindeer instead of Pilgrims or the Thirteen Colonies! Surely, Santa would understand if she came to him for help!

Several miles further, still no encounter with human establishment while the sky started to dim. Anxiety and remorse started to weigh her aimless trudge. She felt lost; she hadn't deliberately run away from home and she was supposed to be grounded. She both worried and pined over getting back now. She'd never lie, fail another test, stay up late, or even do art at home again if any of it got her back where she belonged. She started wandering through a copse that reminded her of the eastern woods she started playing in earlier that day. These woods weren't quite the same, but a warm, golden glow emanated from the other side. Surely, that meant *some* place she could stay! With hope, sheShe hopefully picked up her pace.

Getting closer, the glow burst with the life and color of a rustic village! A train chugged in the distance, a bell tower rang out, and she thought she heard carolers singing. Even warm smells from food vendors or establishments nearby reached Jessie from yards into the shadow of the woods. With the woods finally behind her, she was close enough to see warm-bundled people coming and going and children playing. A horse-drawn carriage full of passengers coursed along too. Gas lamps and building lights lit their cobbled streets.

For the first time in a while, the snow draft Jessie had been chasing slipped up from behind her, carrying a gentle chill in its breeze. It seemed to beckon her to the village. She realized how cold and tired she was and how inviting it looked. She finally quit staring and proceeded to it.

Despite being out in the elements, a warm atmosphere emanated from the edge of town that both dulled the cold and welcomed her in. While treading into the city limits, her mind returned to figuring out where she was. Everything she heard and read was English, so she was at least in a northern English-speaking town-- unless by some magic that was just what she heard. Nothing around looked modern to her but nothing looked like she was among newly-settled pilgrims either; she was somewhere in between. Wherever she was, it was definitely Christmas time though. All over, she saw bows, ribbons, wreaths, and garland adorning doors, windows, walls, and posts. She stopped to stare again when she saw a tall, dressed evergreen in the town square. It was the biggest decorated tree she had ever seen!

Even the branches beyond most normal people's reach were well-dressed with tassels and trinkets; it made her wonder again if she was somewhere magical. She could only imagine how the seemingly-normal people around her managed to decorate the higher boughs! She didn't wonder very long though as she was suddenly jostled off her feet. Some boys were futzing around nearby, slipped on some ice, and knocked her down.

Even for wherever she was now, boys here could be wild oafs too, she thought while on the ground. The oafs were a little bigger and older than her, likely young teenagers. At least they were apologetic when realizing they had an unintended casualty. Albeit the exchange was rather brief as a stern voice nearby reproached them to get back to work. The oafs dispersed but one closer to Jessie's age remained and helped her to her feet.

"Hi, I'm Robbie," The oafs dispersed but one closer to Jessie's age remained and helped her to her feet.

"I'm Jessie. What about you? Do you have somewhere else to be?"

"They were all apprentices in their family trades. I'm not old enough yet, but I wish I was sometimes."

"What for? How old are you?"

"I'm nine. Apprentices usually start when they're

twelve or thirteen. I want to be like my friends' brothers and their friends; they get to help people, go places, or make stuff all day and earn money!"

Another shout cut in their conversation.

"'Ay, jolter-head walker!" It was directed at Robbie this time from an approaching driver of a donkey cart pulling goods, "Pick a side!" Both Robbie and Jessie made way.

"And grown-ups won't yell at me when I'm older either," Robbie sulked.

"I got in trouble in school for something that wasn't even my fault," Jessie added. "The substitute teacher didn't seem to care."

"How rotten."

"What do you want to apprentice for when you get older?" Jessie changed the subject.

"I wish I could drive carriages or trains, but my father is in business. All I see him do is read the paper and make his calculations for profits, dividends, or whatever."

"Can't you be what you want when you grow up?"

"Father says I have to use my skills if I want to make my way in life--whatever that means. He says I have skills in math, but I don't want to sit around all day of my life counting numbers."

"Everyone says I'm a born artist, but trying to do it all day gets me in trouble. In fact, I'm actually grounded because I should've been sleeping or doing homework instead of drawing pictures. I was playing at my grandparents house and somehow ended up here. It's a lovely place, but I don't know where here is."

"You're in Dickensville,"

"Are we near the North Pole at all?"

"I like to think so,"

"Do you think Santa Claus could help me get home? I don't want to get in any more trouble. I'd give up the Ultimate Art Kit if I had to."

"I've been wondering if he could make me a grown-up. Perhaps we could find out together tomorrow!"

"Great idea!"

Before the night was over, Robbie also found Jessie a place to sleep at one of the inns in town. The next morning, they met in the square again to start their journey. They went northward through town, crossing the train tracks, and towards the foothills. Jessie's snow drift swirled ahead of them.

After climbing a hill, they looked down on another village...made of ice and snow!

"Surely, we can't be there already?" Jessie claimed.

"Only one way to find out," They tumbled down the slope, whooping and laughing, and stopped near the edge of the new town.

"Were those snowmen there before?" Jessie wondered

as she got a better look around. The figures stood still, staring at them, gasping and bearing looks of displeasure.

"So sorry to drop in. We came from Dickensville. Is this the North Pole?"

"No." An unhappy snowman curtly answered, "But if you'll put together our friend you knocked over," they gestured with a skinny, stick arm to snow clumps, sticks, and coal rocks surrounding them. "We know someone else who'll help."

Appalled at themselves, Robbie and Jessie scrambled to reform the dismembered snowman, all the while apologizing to the bystanders. None of them softened, as if their emotions were made of ice too. The snow-body started to squirm and mumble as the children gave him shape. He had opinions to voice once they developed his head.

"Haven't you brats ever built a snowman before? My body's too lumpy...I'm too short! My arms are uneven...my eyes are too low...now their too far apart! Here! For heaven's sake, I'll do it!" They did their best to correct the alleged defects, but the grumpy snowman took over when enough of himself was formed.

"Hmph!" He added when he was done.

"Look for the cottage of Nik Saint Stan," the unhappy snowman declared, "He lives beyond town." He pointed through the village, "Please don't wreck anything else on the way out."

Robbie and Jessie nodded and started in the way they were directed. The snowman village returned to its normal routine, save for a few more scowls or wary looks from others they passed. They were sorry about tumbling into the snow-person but just as much they wished they were more welcome to explore their wondrous town. It was much like Dickensville, just with every building and structure fashioned out of ice and snow.

Several miles beyond they found the cottage of Nik Saint Stan. They stood before a normal stone cottage this time at the edge of another wood. A bright glow peeked through a large, frosted-over front picture window and a snow drift peeled off the roof as if to emphasize this is the right place. Cautiously, they approached the door, wondering what to expect.

Their gentle knock was answered by a burly but kind-looking man with grayish-white hair on his head and face. "Well, hello!" He appeared to be someone they knew, but his looks varied just enough for them to second-guess. Nonetheless, the man seemed to know them.

"Are you Nik Saint Stan?"

"I am! Come on in out of the cold!" They obliged and stepped into a cozy living room heated by a blazing fire. Looking around, they saw the fireplace adorned with a wreath hanging above it, garland on the mantle, and a stocking hanging from it. Other than that, Nik's home furnishings were mostly functional; he had some dishes and cookware, a small dining table, candles and lanterns for light, simple curtains in the windows, some wood-working, cleaning, and fireplace tools, and one shelf on the wall with a few books nearby a clean workshop desk. If this was Santa, this The place was far from their expectations of where heSanta would actually live.

"What brings you to my humble abode?" Nik asked, turning from his kitchen space with refreshments for them.

"We were looking for Santa Claus and the North Pole. We have some special requests we were hoping to make. The snowmen at the ice village said to come to you. I never imagined real snowmen being so crabby though."

"They've had a longer winter than usual," Nik explained. "They live better without a lot of heat and sun. They're fragile and like to take their time with what time they have so they're best approached with a bit of caution."

Now they understood why the snowmen were so upset with them.

"If you don't mind me asking," He said, turning his attention to them. "What were you wanting to see Santa about?"

"I wondered if Santa could make me a grown-up?" Robbie started.

"Why, whatever for?" Such a thought perplexed Nik at first.

"I want to be an apprentice and have skills to make my way in life. I won't have that for another four years."

"I'm sure both of you are at an age where it can be hard to be you right now, but the thing about being a grown-up is that you grow into it, get it? Growing is one of the longest things you'll do, but at the same time, you'll be there before you know it! Besides, you'll need that time to grow in your skills as well, so you can be the best apprentice ever, my boy! I've got something for you..." Nik went to his worktable and came back with a snowman trinket.

"Live like the snowmen," Nik said, giving it to him. "Don't rush your life. Those who do wish they could be your age again! Now, what was your request, miss?" He invited Jessie to speak.

"I'm in a bit of trouble," She started. Nik was concerned, but intent. She told him about the trouble she had at school, her punishment, the Ultimate Art Kit, and her concerns about getting home.

"If you think about gifts for a moment, they're often very special. Some you get on a particular occasion or from an important person in your life. Whatever makes them significant, gifts can make life better, don't they? Your passion for art is a gift, Jessie. So, at the right time and with the right people, your gift can be exceptional!

Keep that in mind and your imagination won't get you in so much trouble anymore. Now, remember how I said the snowmen had a long winter?"

Nik directed Jessie's attention to the worktable where crates containers of bright winter and costume accessories appeared. Jessie immediately got it. Excitedly, and carefully this time, they returned to the ice village offering to play dress-up with the snowmen. They were open and even delighted with the children's visit now.

Waving goodbye to the cheerfully dressed snow figures was the last thing Jessie remembered before waking up in the floor next to the Christmas village. She was partly relieved knowing she hadn't left her grandparents' house after all, but also partly baffled as the snow outside looked just like it before she got lost. She didn't dream the future, did she? Turning to survey the Christmas village, she felt a peculiar sense of familiarity with it now: the horse-drawn carriage, the caroling figures, the large, partially-decorated pine tree centering town, a stone cottage on its outskirts. She felt as if she had seen them before, in real life, not as decoration. But her thoughts dissuaded when she was beckoned to the kitchen for breakfast.

She indeed played outside later, working on a snowman in the backyard and staying within sight of the house. Sure enough, the wind cast the rooftop snow towards Jessie's eastern woods. Her curiosity nagged while watching it, but thought better of it just in case.

Jessie returned home at the end of the weekend and her punishment concluded soon after. With Nik's advice in the back of her mind tamed her wild imagination and she did better to listen, obey, study, and take care of herself when she was supposed to. And she received the Ultimate Art Kit for Christmas.

PART 2 - A DANCE

From then on, Dickensville became Jessie's special place. Setting it up was always her favorite decorating task to help Grandma with and she always had new stories to tell through the collection. Her visits there also continued at least once a year, as if being at her grandparents' house at Christmastime with the collection on display was the key to going. When she got there, she'd meet up with Robbie and eventually all the other children of the village as well.

Life there was idyllic, if not a little out of time in Jessie's opinion at first. They didn't have smartphones, computers, television, or video games. Although some had electricity and radio they had electricity, and some had radio. Life there seemed to exist perfectly without those devices and Jessie easily learned to embrace it too. She understood this world a lot more after she learned about Charles Dickens and "A Christmas Carol" in school; the town was named for him and set in his era of history.

The traditions were no different when Jessie was fourteen, but a date to the middle school winter dance preoccupied her mind that year. Boys were no longer so repulsively oafish; they could be cute, but lately they were more so awkward, especially about the event. She remembered falling asleep in her grandparents' living room with nothing but the warm glow of the village lights after setting it up one night, but woke up to the lull of a carriage ride and the sounds of life in downtown Dickensville. The vehicleIt stopped, she got out, and immediately got swallowed up in a fun, gang-like snowball battle involving every young person in town. The opposing side was on the charge, chasing the other team through the streets while smaller groups spread out hoping for cover or to regroup. Jessie trailed behind a couple teammates until a rather aggressive wayward snowball met her face. Stunned, she landed in the middle of the street.

She sat in a stupor, unaware that another carriage was several feet behind her. Before she knew it, she felt scooped up and led out of the thoroughfare.

"Oh gosh! Are you alright?" A worried male voice beside her asked.

"Mmm? Oh! Yeah! Thank you..." Jessie flustered

while turning to face who the voice belonged to. He pulled a familiar snowman trinket from his pocket and she remembered. "...Robbie!" She smiled. He had become one of her best friends here, although her best friend must've grown a lot within a year. His face was more mature than the last time she saw it. It was a few inches higher and on a broader frame wearing a tweed overcoat too.

"Jessie!" He reciprocated, a smile melting his worried expression. "I'm glad to see you!"

"Me too! And thanks again for keeping me out from under the horses' feet!" She laughed.

"No problem!" He chucked as well, whilst examining her cheek, "But maybe we should get you inside for a little bit to make sure that doesn't turn into an ice burn." He took off his own scarf, wrapped it around her, and adjusted it to cradle her face. "How about some hot cocoa from the tea shop?"

"I'd love to!" There were not many circumstances where she'd say no to her favorite holiday drink. The two strolled across town to the tea shop, feeling giddy and suddenly a little shy. Robbie wasn't self-centered but he never expressed so much concern for a playmate before. Plus, Jessie was prettier than he remembered.

Robbie led them to a couple seats near the fireplace when they got there. The firelight and the warming flush in his face drew Jessie's attention to his eyes and his chestnut hair after he took off his newsboy cap.

"What have you been up to?" He asked when they were settled.

"I'm almost finished with eighth grade. I have a dance coming up," He'd make a very nice date if it were at all possible. "What about you?"

"I've just become a bookkeeper with my father's company," Robbie answered. He finally began apprenticing with his businessman father at thirteen and learned the work can involve traveling. He showed a strong aptitude for finance as well.

"Oh!" Jessie was intrigued, "Almost a man now! That explains the nice coat," She smiled.

"Yeah," he sighed. "Father wants me to attend college in the city to gain a more formal study in banking, but if I did, I don't know if I could see you again. I've thought about you a lot lately, Jessie, and I wish I could see more of you than just at Christmas as it is."

"That's the sweetest thing anybody has ever said to me..."

Overwhelming, anxious thoughts trailed her off. Books and tv shows made romantic gestures seem so grand. Now that she was receiving one--with expectations based on what she's watched and read--it was intense to actually experience! Her heart sped up and she almost choked on her sip of cocoa.

All she wanted was a date to her dance... wouldn't he be looking to get married if he's "almost a man"? Is he interested in marrying her?! In this world marrying as teenagers may have been nothing, but she still had high school ahead of her! Even if they didn't marry right away, any other time, Jessie adored the idea of long-time sweethearts. Only if she agreed to Robbie, her sweetheart would be living in this Christmas dreamland. As much as she wished to see more of anybody from Dickensville sometimes, it didn't seem to exist outside of Christmastime.

"--But I just couldn't," was all she could say. Her heart deflated. Who would've thought her desires were unattainable even in her Christmas dreamland?

Robbie sunk as well. Among other things, he very much wanted to understand why he only saw her at Christmastime, but if she did not reciprocate his desires, he only felt it polite not to push matters further. The once-friendly pair now sat forlornly together at the tea shop hearth, broken-hearted in the merriest time of the year. Even the glowing fire now seemed to dim before them.

"Good morning, Jessie!" Her grandmother's voice cut through the atmosphere. Following the direction of the voice to the tea shop entrance, the matriarch hung on the doorframe, glancing inside, as if she herself traveled across town looking for her. The next moment, Jessie was looking at her grandmother from across the living room in their house again. "What would you like for breakfast?" Taking her cue, Jessie started the day.

After that weekend, her grandmother decided to bequeath the Christmas village to her granddaughter. Her grandparents were downsizing, and Grandma felt putting up the village was starting to take more energy than she had, but she took joy in how much Jessie would love taking care of it now. Straightaway, she set it up in her room at home and started to realize a couple things: the Dickensville she experienced in-person seemed to correlate with the set on-hand and it hasn't changed in years. Perusing additions for the collection online, she started to wonder. She bought a Dickensville bank.

One night, she couldn't sleep. Bringing herself to her feet from her bed, one moment she was shuffling across her room, the next she was shuffling into a rather quiet Dickensville. It breathed a low glow, but still a warm glow as if lights were kept on just for her. A lone horse carriage, a lamplighter, and a stray cat trotted the streets with her at first. A snowdrift somersaulted across her path. How late was it?

She wandered towards the center of town, sure

enough passing a bank. She continued to the square where the decorated pine with its trinkets catching the last available light smoldered a late-night afterglow. She saw a lone figure standing on the bridge, looking towards the tree as well. Curious, she approached, and both were extremely surprised.

"Jessie?!" The figure turned when he heard footsteps on the bridge.

"Robbie?!" Jessie immediately recognized him. They ran and embraced each other.

"I'm sorry if my idea earlier was overwhelming," He started. "You're my dearest friend, but I forget you're still young."

"We can still be friends if you'd like," Jessie told him as they let go of each other for a moment. "But distance shouldn't be a problem anymore."

"Absolutely!" Robbie grinned and hugged her again. "Now if I recall," he announced, "you have a dance coming up!" He offered her an arm. She accepted, of course, surprised that he took the hint! He led her to the town hall where Dickensville's own event was underway. She had a date to a dance--much less in her favorite place--and he still had his best friend. Christmas dreams this year were satisfied.

PART 3 - A SKI TRIP

J essie crashed into a metal post trail-marker while skiing.

This predicament all started in her first days of high school. Fifteen-year-old Jessie, lover of Christmas, found a new infatuation: fellow classmate, Greg Hammond. She first saw him about eight lockers down from hers in the first week days of school. He wasn't anyone she went to school with before. He walked right by her one day as he focused on his class schedule and school map, trying to figure out where to go. She should've said something but forgot her manners in her wonder over him. He was lank, but with a hint of muscle growing. He dressed simply but decently in jeans, a tee-shirt underneath a hoodie jacket. His shoes were new, and he looked smart, but not in a nerdy way. She forgot herself still as she ended up trailing behind him in the hall, both of their destinations being a class they had together.

She was with her friends at lunch that day but still in her own world, thinking about him. They asked what was up when finally noticing her lack of engagement in their conversations.

"Have you all seen the new boy, Greg Hammond?" She responded, to which they all had an affirmative answer. One of them said his family just moved to town and all of them were in a class or extracurricular with him. Reading her sappiness, they excitedly squealed and cooed and teased at the realization she liked Greg. Jessie cringed a little; their reaction was rather loud and suddenly she wanted to deny these new feelings. She didn't know anything about him or much less did he seem aware of her existence.

Jessie was in the lost puppy stage for days, noticing how Greg became buddies with the athletes and smart kids. He was part of the pep squad and debate team—not quite her circles, unfortunately. She was more of a quiet, artsy type who got stage fright panic attacks in performance settings and didn't think herself strong or coordinated enough to be part of athletics either. So the months drug on without any progression in talking to Greg.

The long-suffering torch Jessie carried for Greg couldn't dampen her spirit at the start of Christmastime.

It was the season of love, joy, and hope, after all, she thought. In her higher spirits, and inspired by a teen romance advice blog post that encouraged trying to take an interest in a crush's interests, Jessie joined the school's ski club after discovering Greg was involved too. Their first outing was at the start of Thanksgiving break.

"You wouldn't do ski trips for me but you'll do them for a guy?" June, Jessie's best friend and now fellow ski clubber, jokingly balked. "You trip up the steps like every few days, and you want to move downhill. In the snow. With your feet strapped to a board?" June was primarily Jessie's wing-girl for this trip, but of course, she was going to double as Jessie's guide to all things skiing too seeing as her friend had no experience with it.

"I'm getting better!" Jessie defended, "I fall only once a week now! Besides, sometimes I imagine falling into Greg's arms..."

"Gaagghh!" June bleched out with a laugh, "Maybe you will on the slopes this weekend. You've got it bad and *something* needs to happen between you two!"

The club arrived at the resort and purchased their gear if they didn't have any already. As per June's recommendation, the two girls got in line for a ski set that Jessie would use. Several other students were in the same line as well, so Jessie didn't feel terribly out of place, but her heart stopped when seeing Greg saunter through the resort shop with a snowboard. He must be really good at this, she thought.

"Crawl before you walk, Jess!" June's admonishment in her ear broke her dreamy daze, "Ski before you snowboard. That's square one for you. You can get his attention without killing yourself."

They warmed up and geared up and June led Jessie to the bunny slopes for personal basic lessons. "Alright, you're coming along pretty well!" June exclaimed after coaching her friend for a while. "I'm going to take a few runs down the hills but I want you to keep practicing on your own. I'll be back for you in a little bit and we can try something else if you're ready. You need to really have the basics down before even thinking about the proper slopes. Do not leave this training area! Understood?"

Jessie nodded and June left for the bigger trails. She dutifully continued to plod and skid the training slopes and was getting to the point she thought she could manage with her eyes closed. Taking a short break and looking around the ski area, she couldn't help but notice that most of her classmates were shredding the hillside trails. Resigned to the kiddie corner with no other guests obviously over the age of thirteen, she felt deserted. If she was doing so well, Jessie thought to herself, how come June didn't invite her to one of the bigger slopes already? Her mind made up, she plodded to a nearby green trail.

"I'm sure I could be down this one and back before she knows I'm gone too."

The piste Jessie ended up on was a low-grade, gradual curve downhill. She thought she could get away with minimal maneuvering on it. At the start of the trail, she assumed the position and plodded herself forward, letting physics and gravity immediately take over and do the rest.

"Whee! I'm doing it!" She thought several feet in, but her thrill soon switched gears. Her focus was in front of her as it should be, but in her peripherals, she saw an embankment drop on her left. Her fear of heights envisioned a thirty-foot drop-off over it. She leaned to the right to put distance between her and the imagined danger. From one hazard to another, Jessie noticed other skiers and boarders within her direction of travel while her momentum was increasing fast. Uneasily, she narrowly dodged them, but inched back towards the alleged drop in the process.

Before long, the trail widened as other pistes intersected at that spot. The frightening height was gone, but in an effort to avoid the crowds ahead, Jessie made a wrong turn, not realizing she moved into a faster, steeper blue trail. Feeling utterly lost and like she was going 180 mph, she let out a scream, leaning and twisting hysterically trying to slow down or stop, but only increased her lack of control. The only thing that could stop her was a metal post sign marking the trail.

Her consciousness finally registered a voice calling her name. "Good Heavens, Jessie! Are you alright?" Inquiring was "Mattie" Matilda Fisher, Dickensville's tomboy as a little sister to three brothers. *I'm not home and I haven't put the village out yet! How am I here?* Jessie wondered to herself before acknowledging the concerned party. Mattie pulled her up from the ground; skis strapped to her feet here indicated she must've been trying it here too and nearly hit a tree.

"At least the snow buildup around it softened the blow," Mattie exclaimed, "or you'd have a bad bump,"

"Thanks..." wondering if she didn't have one already. "I've had enough for today though," Jessie started working her feet out of her skis.

"Oh, alright", Mattie agreed, "We need to be home before dark anyways." She whistled uphill to summon her brothers before skiing herself ahead into town, a whoop in her voice. She loved adventure; bravery seemed so natural to her.

"How are you so fearless?" Jessie asked Mattie when finally catching up to her.

"I guess because I haven't encountered much that I haven't been able to walk away from and if I ever am in trouble, my brothers or someone to help are almost always around."

Now Jessie regretted not listening to June earlier. Feeling alone was actually the scariest part of her crazy downhill trek.

"What's troubling you?" Mattie turned to her wondering.

"I've never skied before in my life," Jessie admitted, "but I hoped it would help me talk to a boy I like."

"Sounds a bit much," Mattie could be direct too. "Sometimes half the battle with fear is simply doing it."

"I don't know how! He and I seem so different I don't know what to talk about."

"You won't know that for a fact until you try and being yourself is the simplest thing you can do. If it proves true, you can eventually walk away from it; you're not losing a limb to bear-wrestling or anything, but sometimes there's a thrill in proving yourself wrong too."

Mattie's frank views were refreshing. Between that and finally having her own two feet back, Jessie felt grounded in more ways than one; interesting how that happened in her Christmas dream world of all places. Next thing she knew though, she heard her name called again, but from some vague direction at first.

After a couple more times, she woke in the ski resort's medical center with June calling her name.

"I told you not to leave the bunny slopes for a reason!" Her concerned friend chided. "I was going to surprise you...I went to find Greg to set you two up to go down some slopes together! No sooner do I track him down does the teacher find me to tell me you were scooped up off a blue trail and taken to medical!"

"I'm sorry for not listening," Jessie really felt like an idiot now, "and for ruining the surprise."

"It may not be completely ruined," A boy's voice claimed. Greg entered the exam room with a cup of hot chocolate. Jessie was pleasantly stunned. June slid out as he came in, subtly signing her thumbs up and ok's wishing her luck with this endeavor.

"So..." Jessie started. Just do it. *Be myself. Here goes nothing.* "What happened to me?"

"Your face is bruised from the impact," Greg started, handing her the hot chocolate, "and you may be sore for a few days, but impressively, no other serious injuries."

Hmm, he's impressed with me!

"I ran into a sign though, how embarrassing!" Jessie winced at her social mishap.

"I tumbled off a ski lift when I first started out," Greg countered, laughing. "It wasn't a long or hard fall, but it was awkward!" That cheered Jessie up.

"This is really out of my comfort zone," she confessed.

"I'm so clumsy and I'm just more into cooking and art museums..."

"Would you want to go to the one in town when you're feeling better?"

"Really?!"

"Yeah! I was wanting to see the Christmas tree exhibit anyways,"

"I love Christmas!"

"Me too!" Mattie was right; Jessie couldn't be more excited to have proven earlier doubts wrong. She felt empowered. So this is how it felt to be brave. She had a friend's help getting to this point, and eventually, she was simply herself, and in the end, things worked out!

ABOUT KATIE JOHNS

Katharine "Katie" Johns is a college friend of James' and graduated from West Virginia State University with a bachelor's degree specializing in English Education. In her spare time, she is an English and writing tutor, an occasional blogger, and just journals and free-writes any chance she gets.

THE MONSTER IN MY DREAMS

Tony Kreed lives a normal life, with the same schedule. However, out of the blue, Tony has a dream with a creature that makes no sense. He tries to solve his constant, nerve-wracking dreams, but no answers. In desperation, he goes insane, and stops at nothing to stop the dreams. Who would've guessed evil never stops at the mind, but at the soul?

THE MONSTER IN MY DREAMS

By Damian Stevenson

THE MONSTER IN MY DREAMS

I should've listened. I should've known better. As I write my last thoughts and words, heed my warning. Never speak to the man in the bowler hat if you're at the park. Dream or not a dream. I thought I just dreamt it, and...and I'm paying the price for that. I'm not even sure if he's real, or if I'm just stupid. Wrapped up in something I started from a dream? You're probably confused. I get that. Let me explain.

My name is Tony Kreed. I was twenty-six years old when I started this punishment. am from when I started the punishment, twenty-six years old. I worked an office job in Pennsylvania, and lived in Wheeling, West Virginia. Everything was great, really. Just the way I wanted it! All by my lonesome, and the only time people bothered me would've been when I was at work. At least, it was just at work, before I started having these strange dreams. I would wake up on a bench at some park in Wyoming, and I couldn't move my legs. Hell, I couldn't move from my seat! I would watch the sunset clouds drift eEast, and listen to the sounds of birds chirping. I loved it, but there was always something strange about what came next. A man in a suit, along with a bowler hat, would sit beside me. I couldn't make out his face, but...I could feel it. He just...wasn't human. There was no way he was human. His mannerisms, his little fidgets, just his breathing. I just knew it. Uncanny Valley, I call it. He didn't speak, but he would watch me. I could feel it. The burning sensation of prying eyes, eating away at your soul. He wouldn't speak until you spoke first.

"Hello?" I'd say., and then he'd speak. His voice was shallow and whispery. H, and he twitched with every word, his invisible eyes just watching. "My, what wonderful weather we're having. Your thoughts?"

"I...don't mind..."

Then, we'd sit in silence for a minute or so. To break the silence, he would chuckle, and speak. "What is something you want, hmm? A simple desire, made of sweet innocence?."

It would throw out the same question, every night I had have this dream a. And I'd respond the same each time. "I have everything I'd ever want, really."

Then, he would give off this...frustrated-sounding release of breath. "I suppose if that's true, then I have no need for you. I'll see you soon."

Then, I'd wake up. It would drive me crazy. Some nights, I couldn't sleep, hoping to avoid the strange man. People at work would start noticing my strange ongoing-coming irritation. No sleep makes the mind weak, I remember my mother would say. I didn't mean to be rude, or upsetting, but I was so put off by these dreams. Day after day, night after night, I'd research this bowler hat man. The only thing I can ever achieve out of it is a painting called . "The Son of Man" it's called. It looks like that man, but there's no apple dangling from his hat. One morning, at work, so irritated by the same results, I threw my computer. Then, they politely let me go,. A after they tested me for any sort of drugs or alcohol, of course. Then, I went home. I stayed home for a while. My friends from the office would check up on me, occasionally, but I wouldn't have it. No interruptions until I can find this... this dream. Find out what it means. If it is a monster or demon of some sort, why me? Why choose the most unin-teresting person imaginable? Was it trying to break me? To rReveal to the world my true, deepest, darkest desires? If that's the reason, then it's working.

"You hear that, bowler hat man? You've won!" I would shout at the top of my lungs. I dreamed of a world where my life was normal again, w. Where no one bothered me. The night after my neighbors called the police, I had that forsaken dream again. It only bothers me when I least expect it. That's the worst part. The dream only happens when that Son of Man thing feels like showing up. However, in this dream, it was night. I could also finally see the man's grin. His chilling, otherworldly smile. He had no lips. His gums seemed to shoot straight into the flesh where his lips should be. The size of his teeth were also very cartoonish. His eyes, however, did not exist. Just flesh that stretched shot across the sockets.

"Hello, Son of Man."

"My, wonderful weather we are having!" That same piece of dialogue, but he cut it short. I was curious.

I was curious. He cut it short. That same piece of dialogue.

"I feel it now." He said, twitching at the smile, his flesh shaking.. He then started to twitch at the smile, and you could see the flesh shake. His arched smile collapsed and reemerged and then rebuild. "You're hungry." He told me, staring as he always does.

"I'm sorry?" I didn't understand. replied.

"My boy, you desire peace. What would you do for it, Tony?"

His voice shook me to the core. It's a dream. Of course, he'd know my name, but...it still bothered me.

"I'd do a lot for that peace." I told him. That was my first mistake.

He chuckled, and then sighed. "That was a good conversation...Tony..."

Then, I woke up. I wasn't sure why this dream was different, or if it really was a dream. The pure thought of this man was chilling, and now...he's gone off of his known dialogue. It was driving me insane! Eventually, after more failed research, I couldn't keep in my frustration. I threw my phone across the living room, flipped the coffee table, and then I sat there in silence. My throat bubbling, my e. Eyes watering. I put my head in my hands and, and I cried. I couldn't help it.

Maybe...maybe dDeath is the only answer? If I die, then he couldn't bother me anymore. That's what I thought, anyway. I laughed, as I thought I found a way to make him stop. Months, weeks on end, with the same man, *bothering* me. *Pestering* me about my deepest, simplest desires. I just want to be alone. Was that so hard? Why can't the world shy away from me, as if I'm a sick and demented being? That's all I've become, anyway. I walked to the kitchen, and grabbed a steak-kitchen-knife. Or, I should go to the park, I thought. I'll find this man, and I'll make sure he's paid the price. I walked outside, only to discover it was dark. Four in the morning dark. I'm just glad no one's out and about. I don't want them to see what a monster I've become. What a freak this is...nightmarish man has driven me to become. I stumbled my way to the park, in hopes I could find someone, and that's when I saw him. A man in a bowler hat, wearing a suit. I couldn't help but smile. Maybe he'd leave me alone if he couldn't bother anyone again. I charged with my knife, and then he vanished. I launched myself over the bench, and I hit the ground. The knife had plunged into my shoulder. I groaned in pain, pulling the knife out of my shoulder. This wouldn't stop me. I will do whatever it takes to make him stop. To make him get out of my mind. When I stood, covering my wounded shoulder, I laughed. He thinks I'd hurt myself on purpose? I never met a man that couldn't be shot down with any sort of gun. Everyone I know was human. Surely, he could be hurt, too? I walked through the park, watching the shadows. Then, I heard it. In my right ear.

"What is your simplest desire?"

I turned, but there was nothing there. I couldn't help but shake in rage. I started to scream. "Come at me! Show me you are to be feared! Mind games don't work on me!" I kicked the dirt, punched trees, stabbed bushes, but...he never appeared. I fell to my knees and laughed. I'm so stupid. Really, I am. He wouldn't fight me head on. No, far from it. He's breaking me down, mentally and physically. Maybe, just...just maybe, I'm overreacting? Maybe its just a fear I've always had? Deep, deep down, I feared knowing my simplest desires, and he's the only thing that represents my fear.? I took a deep breath, and then I heard a laugh in the forest. I slowly turned my head, and there he was, p. Peeking from behind a tree. He didn't move a muscle. He just...watched me. I walked towards him., and then he hissed.

"Tell me your desires." He hissed.

"What I desire means nothing to you!."

He vanished, and then I was left alone. I shouted again, but...my vision was blurring, m. My head started to throb, and I. I passed out. When I woke up, I discovered that I was strapped to a bed in the hospital. "What...what happened?" I managed to groan. A nurse from outside the room walked in, and smiled. "You were attacked at the park, sir."

"Let me out!."

"Sir, I...I can't do that. Turns out, after some analysis, you have a blood disorder. Hemophilia. That knife was plunged in so deep, sir, that we had no choice but make sure you couldn't move."

"I need to move! I need to hurt him! He's driving me insane!"

I didn't mean to shout. I definitely scared her but . I didn't mean to shout. I closed my eyes and laid back,\ and I apologized to the nurse. She forgave me, but I smiled. I couldn't help it. All I could do was think about that man in the bowler hat. How he's been in every memory I've made without realizing it. The darkness is beautiful. It doesn't lie, it doesn't go away, its paradise to those that crave it. Maybe my desire was to become the bowler hat man? To never exist until you want to. Reality is only as we perceive it, after all.

After a few days, they let me go with a quick mental ability recap test. They said I was dangerous, but not too dangerous. Just avoid knives. I scoffed. I walked back to the park. It was noon this time. I sat on the bench, and held my head. I was looking at the ground , until a woman sat beside me. I didn't know her, I don't think, but she knew me.

"Tony." I turned, and she had a strange twitch similar to the bowler hat man. "We have the same issue."

"No, we don't. Leave me alone. Unless you want me to hurt you."

"What is your simplest desire? Line ring a bell?"

I jumped from my seat and darted home. It was only a ten- minute walk and a five minute run. A run is about five minutes. Avoiding traffic and people, I kept to my thoughts. There's no way he really exists. I sat at home, in a closet. Staying hidden. I heard the front door, creaking slowly. Then, I could hear it. The...the breathing. The shallow breath. My house was still a mess from when I threw everything around, but I didn't care. I had much more pressing matters to attend to. I held my breath, but I heard the lady's voice. "Tony, please. I need your help!. I can't beat him on my own!." I stayed quiet. I struggle enough with him on my own. I don't need to be watching over someone else with the same issue. That was when the closet door swung open, and there she was. "My name is Grace. Nice meeting you, too."

"What do you want?"

"I'm tired of being taunted like I'm a toy. Aren't you tired of it?"

"A little bit."

I couldn't help but stare. Someone with the same problem? Outrageous! I'm probably schizophrenic! This can't be real. "How do I know you aren't him?"

"If I was the Son of Man, I wouldn't have come to you of all people."

"People? There's more of us being haunted by him?"

"Not that I know of, but I know you're struggling."

She offered her hand, and I grabbed it. She was definitely stronger than I thought. She pulled me up, and she looked like me, almost. She hasn't had much sunlight, she's clearly lost weight, and there were are bags under her eyes.

"That creature straight out of a painting, it can't be

killed. I've tried. But However, it leaves once you know its name."

"It has a name?"

And I thought my day could get worse. It didn't. There is nothing more irritating than trying to find the name of a thing from your dreams. Especially since he's following you, w. Watching your every step. We left my apartment, and I just followed her.

"Don't pay attention to him. Never look at him." She'd say. It was hard. He'd appear as a passerby on the street, or maybe even look at us from the roof of a building. From the looks of it, he'd try to reach out to me or Grace, as if he's trying to get our attention, but I won't look him in the face. I won't. Eventually, I got bored of following her blindly, so I grabbed her by the arm and asked her. "Where are we going? Should I worry?"

"Somewhat. We are going to the library."

I didn't question her. That's one of the few places I didn't go to for research. Honestly, I don't know why I didn't think of it. The local library. Maybe there is something about the dream in an older newspaper? Only way to find out would be to search the library. We got there, and the library was empty. As always. You can never find anyone here, except for the librarian. Even then, she doesn't always show up sometimes. Grace and I walked in, and I was astonished. The library was a wonderful sight!. The sun outside mixed with the orange stained glass, giving the entire room a holy glow, and the lightly dusted shelves of near-endless amounts of books stood still. It was like time never existed here. Old things looked better than new and, or vice versa. It all depended on the shelf. The floor was tiled, and certain parts of the library had a velvet colored carpet.

Grace led me up a flight of stairs on the opposite side of the library, and we found ourselves on a small indoor balcony. "I'll use the computer." She stated, and then she pointed to an odd-looking shelf full of old and beaten up papers. "You will check newspapers and documents. Don't argue, because you get mad with the same results." I didn't speak. I nodded, and started digging through the shelves. Grace just typed away at the computer. We spent about thirty minutes looking before the librarian appeared.

"Hello! I don't think we've met." We spent about thirty minutes looking before the librarian appeared. I didn't want to talk to her. My mind was soaring, and I needed to keep it soaring. Searching for something that may not exist would be hard. That's when Grace stood up, her face distraught. "Oh, sorry, ma'am. I meant to tell you we were up here."

"Don't worry about...honey, have you been sleeping?"

"Not very well, but I've been trying. Me and my friend here are just trying to find some remedies for it."

Remedies! What a smart thing to say to someone who isn't suffering. My thoughts were cut short after I could hear his wheezing. His little laughs. I slowly turned to see the librarian was now the thing from my dreams. Grace was on the ground, crawling on her back, and the creature was reaching and walking toward her. Assuming she was in trouble, I threw one of the small books within my reach, and the creature toppled down the stairs it was standing close to. "Grace, are you alright?"

"I'm...I'm fine! The librarian was dead before we even climbed up here! That's why I didn't bother finding the librarian! We aren't supposed to be in here!"

Grace took my hand, and we ran down the stairs. We jumped over the Son of Man, who was now a rotting version of the lLibrarian, and kept running. Eventually, we stopped at the park. At the bench where we first met.

"I'm scared, Tony."

"And you don't think I'm possibly terrified?"

She sat down and started crying. I couldn't help but sit with her. I wrapped my arm around her and closed my eyes. Then, I heard it again. His raspy breathing. I looked up to see him, standing over us. He pulled an umbrella out of his hat, put his hat back on, and opened the umbrella. He held it over us and laughed.

"What is your simplest desire, hmm?"

I stood and grabbed him by the neck. It started raining. For once, I could grab him. My hands were finally wrapped around his cold neck. I couldn't help but scream in rage, and try to kill him. He coughed and wheezed, clawing at my arms. When he stopped moving, I looked up to see people calling other people, some people screaming, then I looked down. I had killed Grace. I turned to the bench, and there he was. He wasn't smiling. The Son of Man had broken. He screamed, and I blacked out.

Back in my bench, in my dream, I met him again. "You failed again, Tony."

"Again?"

"What is your simplest desire, hmm? Something made of sweet, sweet innocence?."

I groaned, and cried. I had killed the only person that could've helped me. "I want to save Grace! I didn't mean to kill her! Had I known-"

He tossed his hat on my lap, revealing hair similar to mine. I stopped crying and wiped my eyes, just to see his hat had an apple in it. "This apple is your only ticket. You look hungry. You desire peace, but what would you do for it? What would you be willing to give up?"

That is what did it. I couldn't contain it. I laughed,

and I grabbed the hat. "Why not become the one thing out to kill me?"

"Is it what you desire?"

"The simplest of desires. I want to save Grace. Bring her back!."

The Son of Man nodded, and stood. "Keep the hat and apple. You will know when to use it."

I woke up, and I was in a police cruiser. Upside down. I looked around, and we were stuck at the bottom of a small valley. The cops were far from living, as I could see one bleeding from the throat, and the other was missing his arm. I was handcuffed, but alright. Just aA few bumps and bruises. I looked around, and I found a green apple in a bowler hat. I picked up the apple, and I cut my finger. Glass was sticking out of the apple on the opposite side. On the side of the apple I couldn't see, glass was sticking out of the apple. I moved closer to the door, and I punched out the remaining glass. I unbuckled, and then crawled out, using my foot to pull the hat out with me. I took a deep breath once I was laying on the ground. I stood, and found a small key hanging from a tree branch about my height from the ground. I grabbed it. the key, praying it opened the handcuffs. and prayed it was the handcuff key., which it was. It was, in fact, the key. Once I unlocked the handcuffs, I grabbed the hat and apple. I put the apple in my pocket, and put on the bowler hat. I knew what I had to do. I climbed up the hill, and the first thing I saw was another police cruiser heading my way. I stood there and covered my face with my hat. I should have payed attention to my location, because I was out in the middle of nowhere. They stopped, and then asked me about what I was doing, just standing there in the middle of nowhere.

"Waiting on someone to clean up the mess down the hill." I answered. One of the police officers opened the door and stepped out of the car. He looked over the hill and grabbed the radio on his shoulder. I shoved him down the hill, and turned to the cop in the driver's seat. "Care to join him?" He exited the car and drew his pistol.

"You're under arrest!" I slowly approached him, hat still covering my face, and my other hand up in the air. I couldn't see, but I could feel him. Hear him, even. "Stop moving, or I will shoot!"

"What is a simple desire, hmm?"

I kept it going. Kept his mind from wanting to pull the trigger. I eventually uncovered my face, and the cop just stared. I tackled him, and then pulled his gun from his grasp. I grabbed the radio on his shoulder, and tore the cord connecting it to the walkie-talkie. I stood, and got in the car. I drove off, and tried to find sa tailor. Someone that could give me a suit. Eventually, I got where I needed to, and found a parking spot. As I was getting out, I put the hat back on. I made sure no one could see my eyes. I walked in, and a small, portly man came around the counter. "Hello, sir! First time?"

"Why, yes, it is. Could you tailor me in a black suit, white undershirt, and red tie?"

"I sure can! That'll be six hundred dollars, but we have payment-"

I drew the gun from the back of my pants and smiled. "I was hoping to get it for free?"

"Oh...um...yes, sir."

The portly man asked me to put the gun down, and he led me to the back end of the store. "You didn't have to rob me of a suit, you know."

"That may be so, but I'm afraid desperate times call for desperate measures."

The portly man just took my measurements, and returned to me with a suit. "You know I'm going to have to call the police, sir."

"Call them in about two hours. That'll be when I'm gone."

The portly man shrugged, and sent me on my way. Whether he If he ever called the police or not when I asked him to didn't matter to me, anyway. I would be long gone by the time they found any sort of remnant of me, my physical body. My physical body. What had happened exceeded anyone's comprehension, anyway.

I went to the park, wearing the suit and hat, and I

ate the apple. Nothing strange happened for a few minutes. For a little bit, I had thought he handed me an ordinary apple, but...that's when I started to feel my lips burning. They had vanished from my face, and my gums took the place of my lips. Then, I found myself at the park in my dream, carrying a suitcase. I walked down the path, and I found myself sitting on the bench. It doesn't seem like I noticed me, which, sounds weird, but how do you explain a situation like this one? I sat down on the bench, and it seemed like I have finally made my presence known. I was thinking about what I needed to say...what I needed to do, but my past -self had spoken first.

"H...hello?"

I had to think about it, and to keep it from being awkward, I said the first thing in mind. "My, what wonderful weather we're having. Your thoughts?"

"I...don't mind."

It was awkward. Just a repeating chain of events. Then, it hit me. I would ease into it. Try to keep me from attacking Grace in the first place, and I'll start by being dodgy with it. "What is something you want, hmm? A simple desire, made of sweet innocence?."

"I have everything I could ever want, really."

I should've known better. I sighed, and I spoke. "I suppose if that's true, then I have no use for you. I'll see you soon." My past-self vanished, and I found myself at the walkway again. I walked on, and I sat down.

Grace walked to me. I turned away, and she spoke. "Hello? Are you alright?" I could barely speak. The only person who could ever help me with myself was her. What she could've gone on to do, but I ended her life. "I'm sorry, Grace."

"Why are you apologizing? How do you know my name?"

"Seek a man named Tony Creed, in West Virginia."

"But I live all the way in Maine! I can't afford a plane, let alone enough gas!"

I stood, and she met my face. From what I could read on her face, she couldn't see anything, but she still met my gaze. She couldn't see anything, from what I could read on her face, but she met my gaze. I grabbed her by the shoulders and screamed. "Find him and help him, or I will make sure you never see Maine again!" She couldn't turn down a monster. Who would? Especially if you could enter minds willingly. She vanished, and I found myself standing alone. I sighed, dusted my suit and hat, and walked off. My suitcase was left behind, but I found myself carrying it anyway. I didn't think anything of it. This world was wild enough, especially for my past -self. What I assumed was my past -self, anyway. I just knew that I could save her. I could give myself a second chance.

For what felt like hours, but turned out to be over two or three months, I made Grace experience the same dream. As for myself, I kept that dream reoccurring. I could see my past -self degrade with every visit. It started with paler skin. Then, it moved on to baggy and red eyes, followed by malnutrition. One morning, I watched as my past -self threw my computer at the office job I remember working at. He was fired, and he went home with a smile on his face, researching what he's going to become. Another few weeks pass, and that's when I had broken my past -self. He started throwing things, shouting that I have won. But I haven't won until I save Grace. He just won't ever understand.

Later that night, since he was still screaming, police were called to his apartment. Our apartment I should say, but I feel as if it makes more sense, as well as make my last thoughts understandable to read. I ended up watching as my past -self grabbed a knife with a smile. I followed him to the park, and I stood in a pool of light from the street-lamps light of the posts throughout the park. I could see that my past -self mustered the courage to charge, and charged me. He didn't get too far, as I stepped out of the way , and he fell over a bench. I heard him scream, and I cringed. I know what happened behind that bench. He fell and plunged the knife into his shoulder. I wanted to help him, but I didn't know how to approach him. He's already sick of me. When he stood and walked around, I stayed hidden. He shouted, and started to attack everything. Eventually, he saw me behind a tree, and I laughed a little bit. The only thing I could do was keep him from going berserk. Just trying to keep him calm. To keep him from hurting himself further. He started to mumble, and I spoke. I had to remind him not to hurt Grace without screwing with time. That was the hardest part. "Tell me your simplest desires."

"What I desire means nothing to you!."

I couldn't believe the answer he gave me. Was I so arrogant? I am trying to help him in every way I can! I've made his presence so known, Grace can find him! That's the only reason I have been haunting him. Then, it hit me. *I* am *his* monster. He doesn't understand I'm helping him. My heart sank, and I vanished. I need to right my wrongs. I found myself in front of Grace, walking around Wheeling. "Hello, Grace."

"Leave me alone!"

She fell to the ground and crawled backwards. I started to reach out to her, trying to get her from running off, but...I failed to do that. I can never do anything right! She got up and ran off, assuming I couldn't catch her. I let her go, and checked on my past -self. What I've been assuming is my past -self, anyway. He was in the hospital. Been a long night. I watched as a nurse diagnosed him with Hemophilia. T, and, thinking about it, I never really cared if I had it or not. It never really bothered me. Though, I was near insanity at that point. Looking on it now, I'd be afraid to even leave the house. Bleeding out from the littlest of cuts caused me a little worry. However, I'm not even sure if I could be hurt anymore. I don't technically don't exist. I followed my past -self to the park once more, where he was sitting on a bench, contemplating previous life decisions. That was when I saw her. Grace. She sat beside my past -self, and started talking. Then, my past -self darted off, and Grace only followed. For some reason, I thought he was running pretty fast, but she kept up with him using a hearty jog. It was a little disappointing. I followed them to the house, and I could see Grace pulling my past -self off of the floor. "That creature straight out of a painting can't be killed. I've tried. However, it leaves once you know its name."

I couldn't help but scoff. I'm a creature? I mean nothing more to them than something they can't kill? It made me a little angry, but then I remembered that I have been haunting them. It's my fault they are this way. They took off to the library., and I tried to grab them, and keep them from repeating the actions I had taken. They just ignored me. Then, it hit me. The librarian is dead! I could use the body temporarily. I took the form of the librarian I had remembered from seeing, and stayed hidden in the library. When Grace and my past -self walked in, they headed straight up the stairs on the other side of the library. I climbed the stairs half an hour after they did, giving them some time to possibly find something, and found them digging through the computer and documents. That's when Grace stood up, her face distraught. "Oh, sorry, ma'am. I meant to tell you we were up here."

"Don't worry about...honey, have you been sleeping?"

"Not very well, but I've been trying. Me and my friend here are just trying to find some remedies for it."

Faking a genuine care was difficult, if not nearly impossible. I couldn't help but laugh at my awful attempt at being an old lady, and I dropped the form on accident. When Grace saw me, she fell to the floor, and then I stretched out my hand to her. After a few seconds of trying to help her, I was hit with a phonebook, sending me toppling down the stairs. I didn't feel any pain, but I didn't realize they had pulled the dead carcass of the librarian out of my soul. I don't even know how I used it, let alone get a hold of it. I didn't think too much more about it, and followed after them the two. A few minutes pass, and I found Grace and my past -self running along back to the park. I don't remember this happening, but I watched Grace and my past -self ram into some person, and I took advantage of this. I let them sit on a bench, and then I approached them with an umbrella from the hat. I prayed he would understand what came out of my mouth next.

, but he didn't get it. "What is your simplest desire?" He didn't get it. Instead, he stood and started to strangle me. Out of fear, I undid the form of Grace, and we swapped places. She was being choked, and I was on the bench. Grace died before my past -self could realize what happened. He looked at the bench, and saw me. I...I couldn't hold my smile. In rage and grief, I screamed, and I found myself in the dreamworld. I was on the bench with my past -self. I didn't even realize what came out of my mouth. "You failed again, Tony!."

"Again?"

"What is your simplest desire, hmm? Something made of sweet, sweet innocence?."

I held my face still. I had failed to save Grace. My past -self then spoke. "I want to save Grace! I didn't mean to kill her! Had I known-" I interrupted him by tossing him my hat. He looked at my head, and he then felt his hair. He must be putting the puzzle together. He found an apple in the hat, and then he looked at me. I spoke yet again.

"This apple is your only ticket. You look hungry. You desire peace, but what would you do for it? What would you be willing to give up?"

That is what did it. He couldn't contain it. He

laughed, and then grabbed the hat. "Why not become the one thing out to kill me?"

"Is it what you desire?"

"The simplest of desires. I want to save Grace. Bring her back."

I nodded and stood. "Keep the hat and apple. You will know when to use it."

I have finally managed to reach him. He disappeared, and I sat on the bench. Without the hat or apple, I can feel my body waning. I managed to find some paper, and I began to write my last thoughts, along with my story. I am writing this story in the world of dreams, but I can feel it out there in reality somewhere. I failed, and I don't think my past -self could ever fix my mistake. However, the world will move on, and I will be stuck trying to save Grace. That's all I've ever wanted to do. She didn't have to die yet, and my insanity has killed her. Time can end when I save her. Until then, the world will have to spin. The Son of Man wills it so.

ABOUT DAMIAN STEVENSON

Damian Stevenson, coming in at the age of sixteen, is the writer of "The Monster in My Dreams". Damian enjoys literature, along with acting and performing in choral arts.

THE GIRL WHO NEVER SLEEPS

Have you ever wanted to live two lives? That way you could experience more and get a do-over? Well, this young girl was able to experience that and more, but it wasn't normal. Instead of sleeping, she would switch between lives. A constant back and forth that was normal for Missy was abnormal for everyone else. Once it was discovered she had two lives, things took a turn for the worst. Join Missy as she navigates her two lives and explores why it is that she doesn't sleep or dream. You might just be surprised by what she finds out.

THE GIRL WHO NEVER SLEEPS

By Lorraine Bradner

INTRODUCTION

I started seeing a psychologist at the recommendation of my school (and my mother making me) about a month ago. Well, one of my mother's at one of my schools. I have one in this life and a different one in my other life. The mother in this life knows that I never sleep. The mother in my other life has no idea because I haven't told her. It didn't seem relevant to that lifeline. This psychologist, like my mother, doesn't believe me when I say I don't sleep. He says that I must be an insomniac who has vivid dreams from the lack of sleep where it causes me to lose touch with what my true reality is. I can talk until I'm red in the face, but neither him nor my mother believe me.

My mother in this life is Sylvia. It's just me and her here. I go to an average school where I get straight A's and

I'm pretty much a loner. I prefer my other life, so I just get by in this one until I switch, which happens when I close my eyes at night. I mean, this is all I've known my whole life. I thought everyone had two lives until my school, Tanser Junior High, called home saying I was spreading lies.

It all started in my 7th grade biology class last month. Our class was learning about sleep cycles in animals and what occurs when animals sleep. A student asked if the animals dream like we do. I raised my hand and asked what a dream was, which right away gave me the outcast status among my peers. They all stared at me confused. The teacher explained what dreams were and questioned me again if I'd ever had one. I said no because I don't sleep. When I go to bed, I wake up in my other life. I explained that I had two mothers, two schools, different sets of friends and I lived in different places. She angrily told me to go to the office and sent a note with me where I got detention. I spoke with the principal, and she told me to stop spreading lies and to think about the nonsense I made up during detention for the next two weeks. I was so frustrated she didn't believe me. I had never even heard of dreams or what this new type of sleep was. My mom was called into the office that afternoon where I told her the same thing, I told my teacher and my principal. I didn't sleep that way. I was either in this life or my other life.

Let's just say, my mother was confused, didn't believe me and had me booked for a session with the psychologist by the next week.

I admit, at first, I was a little worried, but I just shrugged it off. I didn't like this life that much anyways. I'm called Lila in this life. In my other life, I'm named Missy, which I love. I wish I could just stay there all the time, but no matter what I do, I switch lives. Once I got to bed, I switch. I just thought it was normal.

I went to bed that night and woke up as Missy in Sunny Grove, Texas with my mother and father, Therese and James. I have no siblings in this life nor my other one, but here it was warm, sunny, and I had a full family that never fought and was full of love. I'm in was in 7th grade in both timelines. Here I go went to Oaks Junior High. I have lots of friends who I slept over with all the time. Sleepovers are our favorite. I decided, as Missy, to not mention my other life, like when I'm Lila. I don't want to mess up both my lives up. This time when we talked about dreams in class, I just went along and didn't ask any questions. I fit in here. I loved it.

The only thing I have in this life that's a little odd are the sensations that would occur in my hands and hair. Sometimes when I was doing nothing, or just sitting in class, Ii would feel like something was stroking my hand or like wind was blowing through my hair. Once I recall i even felt a tingling sensation on my cheek. Once again, I didn't say anything for fear of being punished. That's one good thing about this magical thing only I seem to experience. I get to redo my days. I got to spend Tuesday, May 15th as Lila in Fort Wayne, Indiana. and I today I got to redo the day, on Tuesday, May 15th in Sunny Grove, Texas. The days aren't exact in each life. The food in my Missy life is better, I get to do sports here and I have tons of friends. In my Lila life, we get to learn more advanced subjects in classes, which is about the only thing I enjoy here.

I was sad to get up as Lila today. The last two weeks have been annoying and confusing. The psychologist thinks I've been lying about not dreaming and sleeping. I don't believe them and they don't believe me. In the back of my mind, I feel like maybe they are right? Still... when I really sit down and think about how my days go, it just doesn't make any sense. There's no time for it. The doctor suggested that my mother put me on medication to help me "dream" and sleep, but thankfully she denied that because the effects of the drug can stunt my growth and she didn't want it to hurt my body in that way. I was already the shortest in my class and that would have just been torture to be stuck like that.

So instead of the drugs, the doctor suggested a different method. He told my mom to buy a camera to set up in my room to record me while I slept to prove that I did in fact sleep. She agreed. We went to the local hardware store, Toolies, and picked up a night-vision camera that had night vision so it could see me if I slept. My mom says she's seen me sleep, but again, I just don't believe her. She set it up last night and we brought it with us today for my appointment. I'm curious but also scared of what we are going to see. The psychologist pulled over his laptop from the table that was right next to him and plugged in the side of the camera to it.

I closed my eyes and took a deep breath. He turned the laptop towards us and pressed play as he stood up to come behind us and watch as well. We watched as I laid down and covered myself with the sheets. I couldn't believe what I saw. I was sleeping. I was staying there in bed, tossing and turning in my sleep. I didn't disappear into my Missy life. The psychologist pressed the speed button to make it go faster and we watched the whole eight 8hours that was on camera. My mom came in a couple of times on the camera, bringing with it a sliver of light that showed I was still in my bed. I was still in this world. F for the entire eight 8hours. I even mumbled in my sleep! I couldn't believe it.

Then my Lila mom, Sylvia came in at 6 am to wake me up. I was still Lila, which didn't make any sense because I was Missy yesterday. Not Lila. I switched lives.

Why isn't it showing it? My head was spinning. I was so confused. Why is all of this happening? My lives were so normal until all of this started up. Why did we have to learn about dreams? I put my head in my hands and tried to shut my eyes, making me switch to Missy. I didn't want to be Lila anymore. How do I stop switching? The psychologist shut the laptop and went and sat down in front of us. Mom grabbed my hand and started caressing it gently and lightly rubbing my back. That always helped a little, but it didn't do much today.

"Well, Lila," the psychologist said. "What do you think? The tape showed you sleeping. It showed that you stayed in your bed the whole night and your mom came and woke you up."

I looked up at him. "I can't explain it. I thought I didn't sleep. When I go to bed at night and shut my eyes, I wake up in another life. I've told you and mom this over and over. The tape confuses me, but it does show something different than what I experience. When that tape showed I was sleeping, I was in another life. I lived an entire day as the other me, Missy. I swear. I don't know what's going on. I don't know what's going on!"

I started screaming and crying. Wishing that this would all just go away.

I shouted, "Mom, I am telling the truth!". I shouted, I don't know what's happening to me!" My mom held me and tried to calm me down, but it didn't help. I tried getting away from her. I wanted to run away. I wanted to go to my bed and shut my eyes and be Missy already. I finally pushed her away and headed towards the door to run home when I felt something sharp poke me in my neck. I felt a prickling hot sensation run all the way down my spine and through my body. Slowly the world began to move underneath my feet. I closed my eyes.

MISSY

I open my eyes, gasping for air and fall out of bed. I look around in a panic. I'm in my purple and green bedroom. I'm in my Missy life. Thank goodness! I slowly crawl up off of the floor and dig my toes into my plush green bedroom carpet. It slowly calms me down. I've decided that I'm not going to go to my Lila life anymore. I'm never going to shut my eyes at night again. I will stay up forever. I can't go back there. I'll do whatever it takes.

I get up and grab my clothes to go take a shower. I was drenched from sweating as Lila. It must've been whatever they injected in me. After I jumped out of the shower, I headed downstairs to have breakfast with my favorite mom and dad, Therese and James.

"You ok, honey? You look a little pale, and I thought I

heard you fall out of your bed this morning." My mom stroked my hair gently. Even after she stopped to hear my response to her question, it still felt as though she was rubbing my hair. It was a nice feeling.

"Yeah, I just got out of bed clumsily, I guess." I hugged her and sat back down to eat my breakfast. My stomach felt a little off, but maybe it's because of that injection. Although, Ii've never had anything transfer lives before, so maybe it's just a weird morning for me.

I got on the bus and went to school like every normal day. My school here is St. Thomas's school for girls. We have matching pant suit uniforms that we have to wear everyday that are in all black. I like it because I never have to try and figure out what to wear. I'm under enough stress these days. I get to class and sit down, drumming my thumbs somewhat anxiously for what we'll be learning today. I hope it's not dreams. The teacher begins talking about the cycle of birth. I sigh with relief. No dream talk this morning. Now to get through the rest of the day. By the end of 8th period, I was finally feeling at peace. This day was going to be normal. Now i won't ever close my eyes long enough to become Lila again. I'll be Missy forever, no matter what it takes. The school bell rings to signal the end of the day. I get up, gather my things and head out the door to go meet my friend Jessie at my locker. She's one of my best friends here. We meet at my locker in the morning and at the end of the day this year since we aren't in the same classes this time.

"Hey Jessie!" I said as I approached my locker.

"Hey Missy! Oh my gosh, how crazy was that sex education talk in Miss Wilkinson's class today. All of us got in trouble for laughing and kept flinging condoms across the room at each other." I giggled as I set my books inside my long blue locker. I have a small mirror in the door of the locker along with stickers from our favorite show, Tyke's Grand Adventures. It's Jessie and I's favorite show about this guy that takes classes of kids on field trips and they get to travel to all of these cool places and learn about survival skills and nature. We've put our school's name on the show's website so many times we've lost count, but we haven't been chosen yet for an adventure. We figure if we keep applying every day, we'll get picked by the end of the school year. We have eleven months to go until the school year is over, so we have a pretty good chance.

"I'm so jealous. My class is so boring. Everyone just sat and listened and didn't make a sound. When she handed us condoms, I giggled a little bit, but Cynthia who was sitting right next to me gave me a nasty look. She's such a teacher's pet." I rolled my eyes and grabbed the edge of my locker to shut it; but before I could, I saw something in the mirror in my locker. I did a second take.

There was nothing but me staring back at me in the mirror, but I could have sworn I saw a nurse in it behind me at first. Must still be trauma from my Lila life. I shut the locker door and walked with Jessie out to the school bus. We took a seat next to each other and gossiped about boys and our favorite show the rest of the way home. My stop is before Jessie's, so I gave her a hug goodbye and told her I'd see her tomorrow.

I got to the front of the bus and readjusted my backpack. I slowly stepped down the stairs and fell face first out of the bus. My feet went numb! I couldn't feel either of my feet all of a sudden. I fell out of the bus and onto the pavement, skinning my arms and knees. The bus driver took his seatbelt off and jumped down the stairs to make sure I was alright. Jessie was right behind him. I started tearing up from embarrassment and pain. He helped me up and asked if I needed help walking to my front door. I shook my head.

"No thank you, sir. Jessie, can you help me? I was just being clumsy.", I quietly replied as I sniffled. My feet were still super tingly like they were just asleep but I had enough feeling in them to walk slowly to the porch with Jessie's help. The bus driver pulled away once we got to the porch. Tears were slowly rolling down my cheek.

"Are you ok, Missy? That was so crazy! I've never seen you be THAT clumsy". We got to the porch and sat down on the first step. I wiped my forearms on my shorts to get the dirt off and started massaging my feet.

"Jessie, my feet went numb. I couldn't feel them all of a sudden. It was terrifying!." She gave me a hug.

"I can stay with you until your mom gets home. She'll know what to do when we tell her what happened. Are your feet better now?" I poked my feet. I nodded my head.

"Yeah, they are almost back to normal now. I don't know what happened. I don't want to worry my mom though, so let's just not say anything to her for now". Jessie shook her head and said we should still tell my mom but I told her no. I don't want to talk to any more doctors for a while. The one I dealt with in my Lila life was enough for a lifetime. It was probably just from that drug they injected in me that made my feet go like that. It had to be.

Jessie stayed with me until my mom got home and thankfully she didn't say anything to her. After she left, mom started getting dinner ready for when dad gets home.

"How was your day, sweetheart?" she said as she shuffled around the pasta steaming in the strainer. It was spaghetti night.

"It was good." I lied.

"Well, good. I'm glad to hear it." She smiled at me after she talked and continued making dinner. I got up and set the table. When I laid the last plate down is when dad walked in. I love greeting my dad when he gets home.

"Dad!" I happily ran to him and was about to give him a big hug when that feeling hit me again. This time it was worse. My feet went numb and I felt a tug. Like someone just tugged on both my feet and pulled them down past the floor. Then I felt a sharp pinch in the back of my neck. The pain was so intense, it caused my vision to blur. I fell on the floor, while shouting, and crying and holding the back of my neck. Mom dropped the pan she had in her hand and came running in to help me. Dad rolled me on my back and was asking me what was wrong. It was so hard to see.

Suddenly, it all stopped again. I could feel the tingling back in my feet like last time. Only this time they felt like tingly boulders attached to my legs. My neck felt completely normal again. "What is happening to me?", I quietly say out loud as tears run down my cheeks. My mom and dad hug me and start talking to each other about taking me to the hospital. I begged them not to take me but eventually I gave in. My dad carried me out to the car while I continued crying. After ten 10 minutes, we arrived at the hospital. I had stopped crying at this point, walking .I walked in holding my mom and dad's hands. The nurses showed me to a room while they started doing tests. It was 10 pm by the time the nurses did their tests and the doctor talked to us. By the time the nurses had been done with their tests and we had talked to the doctor it was 10 pm. I was exhausted, but I was determined not to shut my eyes so that I didn't become Lila. Even after this experience, I refused to go back to being her. Finally, after a bit, the doctor came back in.

"Well, her results all seem fine. All her levels are normal, and she doesn't seem to have any pain currently. That being said, I would like to keep her overnight just to watch her and to run some more tests. I want to order a brain scan so that we can see if there's some abnormal activity going on or to see if this was just some sort of panic attack. I'll have the nurse show you all to your room shortly."

The doctor walked out. I twiddled my thumbs nervously. I've never had a brain scan before. I was a little scared of it.

"Do brain scans hurt?" I asked my dad. "No, honey. They are completely harmless", he said back to me. He gave me another hug. Again, I felt like wind was blowing through my hair, but that wasn't anything abnormal. They took me out of the exam room and led us down the hallway to where the testing was going to happen. The testing room was huge. The nurse had my dad wait outside of the room where I could still see him through the room's windows. They put me in the machine to get the brain scan. It was a big circular tube where the inside of it almost touched my nose because it was such a tight fit after they locked me in. I had to shut my eyes to handle it. It was so scary. I heard a whirring as the machine must've started up. Suddenly, I felt a strong pull on my head. It felt like someone was trying to pull my head off by pulling on my neck. I started screaming. I couldn't open my eyes. Darkness was all Ii saw.

LILA

Everything went quiet. I sat up fast, breathing heavily and opened my eyes. I expected to hit my head on the machine, but instead I didn't. I was in my room. My Lila life room. UGH! How did this happen? There's no way I could've fallen asleep in that machine. It was so painful! I do not want to be back here. My mother knocks on the door and comes in. Sylvia looks tired.

"Hi sweetie, how'd you sleep?" I rolled my eyes.

"I didn't. You know that. Or did you tape me in my sleep today to go over with the psychologist again." She looked down at her hands.

"Listen Lila. I kept watching over you last night, but I didn't tape you again. You were sleeping in the bed as you are every night. You were tossing and turning like you were having a bad dream, but you wouldn't wake up when I shook you. I tried everything to get you to wake up. I put a cool washcloth on your face, shook you, picked you up. Nothing worked. It was terrifying. Then you started screaming so I ran to call the doctor. That's when I came back in and you were awake."

I stood up and walked towards her. "What do you mean you called the doctor? You called my psychologist?" I folded my arms. She looked down again.

"Yes. They are sending a specialist to come pick you up. They want to make sure you are ok, but in order to do that they have to watch over you while you sleep and run some tests. They are going to take you to their sleep clinic where you'll be for the next week." My heart dropped.

"WHAT!?" I screamed. I pushed her aside and ran towards the door. I was going to run away. I was going to figure out a way to never come back here. I reached the hallway and turned the corner. A large man was standing there all in white.

"She's running!" I heard my mom scream. Before I could turn back towards my room, the man grabbed me roughly on the arm. I tried to shake his grip, but he was too strong. He started dragging me towards the door to go outside. I couldn't believe this. I couldn't believe my mom agreed to this. She's a monster. My other mom, Therese, would never do this to me. I haven't done anything wrong. I just don't dream!

"Mom!" I screamed. "Mom, how could you let him take me?! Help me! He's hurting me!" I screamed in between sobs. I felt like I was choking on air trying to catch my breath between all the screaming and crying. At this point, I wasn't on my feet anymore. The large man in white had adjusted his grip and was dragging me by my shoulders with both of his arms. My heels were grazing the carpet down the hallway. I flailed and tried to regain my footing so I could try and push off in the other direction, but to no avail. I attempted to headbutt him by throwing my head back, but he was much too tall for that. When I tried to headbutt him it felt like it bounced off a padded wall which was only his stomach. My heels popped up over the entryway out of the door and down the sidewalk,. My heels were scraping off on the pavement. I couldn't see where he was taking me.

"Mom!" I screamed with all my might. She was standing in the doorway staring at me. Tears were streaming down her face. The man pulled me sideways and positioned me so I was facing this white van. I put my feet up on the back doors where he was trying to shove me. I was pushing myself away from the van with all my might.

"Varl!" I heard him yell. "Help me out here. This kid's

a nightmare". Another man came from around the side of the van. He was holding a syringe.

"No! I screamed. No!" I fought as hard as I could to get away. I was not going to be injected with that stuff again! The large man grabbed me in a bear hug and forced my head down into his shoulder exposing my neck. I felt a stab in my upper spine and darkness came again.

WHO AM I

My eyes felt impossibly heavy. Who am I now? I hope its Missy. I hear a distant beeping in the distance. It's steady and. It's constant. My body feels like rocks. Why can't I move? I try to wiggle my toes. Nothing. I try to move my arms. Nothing. A minute goes by. Suddenly, my feet start tingling. Its the same sensation I feel when Ii'm Missy after my feet go numb. I must be Missy! I relax a little bit. I'm safe. The tingling went away. I wiggle my toes. They're moving! My body still feels extremely heavy but at least i'm feeling again. I wonder if it was that brain scan that did this.

I hear someone shout. "Baby! Her toes are wiggling! I think she's going to wake up! Come here. I'll press the call button for the nurse to come in. The treatment worked!"

That voice sounded like my dad. It's James. Why's he talking like that to mom? What treatment are they talking about? I try to speak but only a mumble comes out. I feel a soft tussle in my hair. It was the same sensation I get when I'm Missy. That feeling that a soft breeze is caressing my hair. This time it felt different though. It felt more solid. I could feel fingers running gently through it.

"Baby girl, it's ok. Momma's here." I felt a kiss on my forehead and a hug. I groan again. Why can't I talk? This is weird.

"Nurse Polly, she's awake! She's finally awake! Tell Dr. Treager the treatment worked. She's back with us."

Ok, this is too weird. What is my dad talking about? I've got to open my eyes. I fight with all my power to get my eyelids to move open. Success! At first, I only saw a little bit of light from the bottom of my eyes. It gets easier as my eyelids slowly slide open. Everything's blurry. Odd. I blink a few times and can see a little better. I turn my head slowly to the right and see my dad. He's crying. I look back left and see my mom crying as well. I want to reach out to them, but my arms won't move much. I can only get them to wiggle a bit when I try.

"Sweetie, do you know what happened? Do you know where you are?" My mom asked me. A nurse came up to me. She starts checking my vitals. I must've really not handled that brain scan well. I croaked again trying to talk. My throat is so dry and a bit sore, like I. Like i haven't spoken in years.

I managed to mumble out, "I was getting a brain scan. Right"? Mom looked at dad a little concerned. Dad grabbed my hand.

"Sweetie. We were in a car accident six months ago. He starts crying again. Your sister... she didn't make it. You almost didn't. To save you, we had to put you in a lucid state coma. It was a dream-like state to keep you alive while we let your body heal. It was only supposed to be for a week, but you never woke up. We did everything we could to get you to wake up, but you just wouldn't." He squeezed my hand. I try to sit up but I can't find the strength to. I start to panic.

"Her heart rate's increasing. Dear, try to breathe and remain calm. I'll go get some morphine to calm you down. Your body is probably in shock," I heard the nurse say. I took a good look at her face. It was my Lila Mother Sylvia! What is going on!? I lift up my head slightly but the pain in my neck was too severe.

"Darling, stop trying to move. It's ok. The doctors have been trying a new treatment. They've been doing neck stretches, feet movements and injecting a new drug into your spine. We just started treatments last week and now you've woken up and come back to us." Well, that would explain what I was feeling as Missy, if what she is saying is true.

"Who's my sister?" I looked up at her, wondering what she was going to say.

"Lila". She whispered. My breathing started increasing again. "We know you're confused, Missy. They said that would happen. The dream state isn't supposed to last this long."

"I was dreaming". I said out loud.

"Yes, dear. You've been dreaming for 6 months. We've been monitoring your brain activity." My head started to spin. No way is this real. Have my two lives been a dream? Am i able to dream? Do i only have one life? My breathing increases. It's getting shorter. Nurse Polly, who I knew as Sylvia, walked in with a large man all dressed in white. Behind him was a man that looked like the Varl I had met. He had a syringe. My mother lifted my head up exposing my neck. I tried to move my body so i could get away. I didn't want this. This isn't real.

"Honey, stay calm, ok? This is just going to help you relax." My mom said. It was no use. I had no strength to fight it. I felt a sharp pain. Darkness overcame me again.

I opened my eyes. I was in a white padded room. No longer a hospital. I shut my eyes again. I was in my Lila room. I shut my eyes once more. I was back in the hospital. I was flickering through each life in seconds. Another sharp pain hit me in my neck. Darkness came again. Darkness became a cycle. My breathing was slowing down. I was beginning to feel numb all over. Heaviness was overtaking me more than I've ever felt. I was relaxed. I felt at peace. Darkness took me over. Darkness was all I saw forever. My sleep finally came at last.

The beeping in the hospital hit a constant tone. Everyone in the room went silent. Missy had passed on. The treatment failed.

ABOUT LORRAINE BRADNER

Lorraine Bradner, Author of 50 Ways to Be Petty and The Heart Healer, received their Masters Degree in Toxicology from the Michigan State University. Watch out for more from this young author as she is only just getting started in her writing career.